THE FAIRY BRIDGE TROLL

THE SEATTLE TROLLS TRILOGY: BOOK THREE

LEAH R CUTTER

BOOK VIEW CAFE

The Fairy Bridge Troll
The Seattle Trolls Trilogy: Book Three
Copyright © 2017 Leah Cutter
All rights reserved
Published by Knotted Road Press
www.KnottedRoadPress.com

ISBN: 978-1-61138-701-8

Cover Art:
ID 21382917 © Prometeus | Depositphoto.com

Cover and interior design copyright © 2019 Knotted Road Press
http://www.KnottedRoadPress.com

Come someplace new...
If you'd like to be notified of new releases, sign up for my newsletter.

I will never spam you or use your email for nefarious purposes. You can also unsubscribe at any time.

http://www.LeahCutter.com/newsletter/

The Clockwork Fairy Kingdom

The Clockwork Fairy Kingdom
The Maker, the Teacher, and the Monster
The Dwarven Wars

The Chronicles of Franklin

Franklin Versus The Popcorn Thief
Franklin Versus The Soul Thief
Franklin Versus The Child Thief

Contemporary Fantasy

Siren's Call
The Immortals' War
Circle of Air

CHAPTER 1

Christine strained to lift the jagged rock and set it into place. Her muscles trembled as she brought the huge boulder skyward. She could see where the rock went, where the edges on the piece she held matched the broken companion already set in place.

Under her left palm, she felt magic pulse through the sigil burned into the rock. It was the troll royal sigil. It looked sort of like a lopsided treble clef: instead of a line going up the middle of the swooping lines, it started to the right then came down on the left.

However, the rock defied her. Somehow, like a child who didn't want to go to bed or a cat who didn't want to be picked up, it managed to multiply its weight.

Maybe if Christine got all the way under the other rock, she could just lift it up…

Christine took a step. Her foot slid. Mud squelched beneath her rubber boots. Christine tottered to the side, a sudden downpour of rain blinding her.

The rock went down hard, splashing mud back up on

her already wet jeans. She did a crazy dance, banging her shin against the rock while flailing her arms, trying to stay upright. Finally, she came to a halt a few feet away.

Christine bent over, bracing herself by putting her filthy hands above her knees on her already disgustingly dirty jeans, panting. Why wouldn't the bridge go back together?

She looked down with dismay at the front of her bright blue waterproof jacket. Before the changeling spell had been broken, she never would have worn something so colorful. Now, she found these colors suited her. Particularly during a wet, cold Seattle February.

However, her jacket, too, was now covered in mud, as if someone had just thrown a huge slush ball and had smacked her right in the middle of her chest.

Christine was going to have to wash everything she wore. Again. She didn't have the money to keep going to the Laundromat!

Though her mom would be happy enough if Christine showed up with yet another bag of dirty clothes. Not because her mom liked doing laundry—she just pointed toward the laundry room when Christine arrived, and Christine did her own work.

But Mum was determined to keep a steady relationship with her daughter. Even if her daughter wasn't human anymore. And wasn't technically her daughter.

After another few deep breaths, Christine pushed herself upright and made herself look back at her project.

Small earthworks, maybe eight feet tall, held the two ends of the bridge. The stones reached across the gap like broken fingers, shattered in their grasp. But despite how the two ends strained to reach each other, a large gap remained.

It felt to Christine as if her progress on rebuilding the fairy bridge was always one step forward, three steps back. She'd barely made any headway this month, despite coming here almost every night after she'd finished work.

The stones that had connected the bridge to the earth on either side had been more forgiving. They'd reattached to the remains of the existing bridge without as much effort—possibly because her earth power had grudgingly helped.

However, the bonds holding the first stones had turned out to be too weak. Christine had had to reseat many of them, then rebuild the magical ties that connected them together.

Just when she felt as though she had the hang of things, the nature of the rocks had changed. They didn't want to go together at all, and she found she needed different spells to hold them in place, magics she could barely manage. At least Tina, her human doppelganger, had been around to help Christine figure out the new spells.

Tina's parents, or rather, the humans who had raised her, Mr. and Mrs. Zimmerman, had been ordered by the court to help Christine rebuild the bridge. But they stopped coming as soon as their appointed sixty days were up.

Christine knew if she went back to the court and complained that they did sixty consecutive days, as opposed to sixty days of actually working, that she could get them to help again.

It wasn't worth the effort.

Her own parents came by when they could. Her brother Dennis as well. But they were merely human, and really couldn't help much.

Christine knew she was doing something wrong. But what?

The bridge still looked like something from one of those disaster flicks, or maybe a daring cross for some motorcycle rider. Jagged edges of stone stuck out from either end, reaching into the empty sky, like lost lovers forever apart. Orange clouds hung in the sky, reflecting the city streetlight, rainy tears mourning the broken bridge.

Christine shook herself. It wasn't like her to get so sentimental about things.

But she had to finish the bridge before she could journey to Trollville. Before she could free her bio-dad from his wrongful imprisonment. Before, well, she could start the next phase of her life. She felt like she was in limbo. Neither here nor there.

Like the bridge.

She hadn't meant to destroy it. But her air power had been trapped within it. The only way to free the element had meant tearing the rocks apart.

Though that hadn't all been Christine. Ming, the demon who'd bound her powers, had ensured that when she retrieved them, maximum damage would be done to the place where each power had been imprisoned.

Why? It was one of the many questions Christine still had.

Some of the answers lay on the other side of that bridge. If only there were an easy way to fix it!

Christine sighed, dragging her feet as she walked back to the pile of rocks under the bridge. Maybe she could find a smaller piece that went in next. Just a chip, so she could feel as though she'd done *some* good tonight and not completely wasted her time. She had a regular job as an archivist at the main Seattle library downtown. And she had no training in building anything, though she'd read as many books as she could find, and studied as much as she could about bricklaying and stonework.

She stubbornly came to the bridge and put in an hour almost every night. Even the time it snowed, in January, about a month earlier.

Christine stared at the rubble in front of her. Where was a piece she could use? What went together where?

She poked at her magical elements, seeing if one of them at least could help her, but they were strangely mute. Sure, sometimes her air element would help her lift things, and occasionally her earth element would turn the rocks more solid. But mostly, they let her work on this on her own.

Did this bridge make them uncomfortable? Since they'd all been trapped in similar places for twenty-eight years? Waiting until she grew up and could rescue them?

After another minute or so, Christine picked up a much smaller rock. Maybe she could just pound it into place…

"Hey there," came a strange voice over Christine's shoulder.

She turned abruptly, the rock raised as a weapon, then relaxed. It was merely Nikolai.

Still—she had an illusion spell going. Or she'd thought

she'd had it up. So humans (and everyone else) couldn't see her, wouldn't marvel at how strong she was, wouldn't ask stupid questions about the work she was doing.

She double-checked the illusion spell that made her at least appear human, instead of as her great, green troll self. She could see both the illusion and her real body when she held up her hands, a shadowy, darker-skinned human hand wrapped around the solid reality of her, though the real her had tough, greenish troll-skin and long white claws. She opened and closed her mouth once. Yup, she could still feel the huge tusks growing out of her lower jaw, as well as her jagged teeth.

"Whoa, whoa!" Nikolai said, raising his hands as if he was giving himself up. "I didn't mean to startle you."

Christine peered at the tiny wooden man. She had *never* seen the shopkeeper outside of his store before. "What are you doing here?" she asked. She lowered the rock but she didn't put it down.

Though if it came to a fight, Nikolai would wipe the floor with her magically.

Probably.

It would depend on whether all her individual magical elements—water, fire, air, and earth—decided to help her or hinder her.

Nikolai blinked owlishly at her. It was always a wonder how much expression he managed on his wooden face, especially since his features were painted on.

Christine had enough magical experience now to see that a lot of his gestures and expressions were magically enhanced. The spell that enabled the wooden man to express himself emotionally was subtle and complicated. It also modified his actions so that he appeared to be using the same body language as the being he talked with.

She had watched Nik shout and pound the counter when giants came walking into Nikolai's Magical Emporium, greeting the giants how they would greet each other. At the exact same time, it had seemed to her that he'd just nodded and smiled, as he would with a human. It had been one of the weirdest experiences Christine had had so far as a troll, and that was saying something.

Nik wore his usual Seattle-grunge-like outfit, with a red-and-black striped flannel shirt, jeans, and leather boots. (Did he have feet? Were the toes fully articulated like his hands? Or did he just have sticks in his shoes?)

She wasn't surprised to see he wasn't wearing a jacket. She was pretty sure that he didn't feel heat or cold like a flesh-and-blood creature.

He barely came up to her chest when she was in human form. Now, she dwarfed him. She felt like a towering mountain faced with a Ken doll.

"I came to see your progress," Nik said. He still held his hands up. "You've made some."

Christine snorted at him. "Not enough."

Nik pressed his lips together and nodded. "Can I see?"

"Yeah, sure," Christine said. She finally lowered the rock she'd been holding. Before she could throw it back on the pile, Nik said, "Could I see that, too?"

Curious, Christine offered it to him.

The rock looked huge in his two wooden hands with the finely made joints. Christine had always been larger than Nik. When she worked on the bridge, she tended to expand even more, her muscles bulking out to match her labor. She also grew slightly taller as well, so she could more easily reach the bottom side of the bridge to place her rocks.

"Here," Nik said. He showed Christine the rock. It looked like all the other rocks, with the royal sigil burned into one side of it. "See, you keep trying to put the rocks together as you saw them, with the sigils facing out."

Christine nodded. Yes, she'd been trying to do exactly that, to remember how the bridge had looked the last time she'd seen it, and then put it together just like that.

"The sigils were burned deep inside the rock when the bridge was first built," Nik said.

He climbed up the side of the hill until he could reach where the bridge started. He balanced there, and then reached up and smoothed his hand over the stones there.

The sigils disappeared from sight. A soft sigh, tinged with relief, wafted through the air.

Christine stared critically at the section Nik had touched. She had to admit that it looked stronger, now. She walked up beside him and ran her palm over the next section of stones, using her earth power to push the sigil deep inside the stones.

They also sighed and strengthened.

"You can't force the rocks to show their power. They carry it deep within themselves. Like you," Nik added.

That made sense to Christine. Why hadn't someone else told her this? The Zimmermans could have offered help like that!

Did they want her to fail? Probably. Because in Trollville, there might be evidence that the Zimmermans had more knowledge of her beginnings, that they'd known they were using a princess for their changeling.

Christine took the proffered rock from Nick. She turned it in her hands so that the sigil faced outward, away from her and her palm. Then she lifted the rock, as if in offering, to the jagged part of the bridge.

The rock in her hand also sighed as it joined the others. It felt much more right to put the stones together this way.

With her other hand, Christine quickly called up her earth element and joined the rocks together.

Finally! They felt solid. Complete.

Maybe she could make better time now…

Nik nodded, as if reading her thoughts. "This won't solve all the problems you've been having. There are other tricks. I can see it, but I don't know how to help, beyond the most obvious of points."

"Thank you," Christine said. "You were a big help." If only he'd come by sooner!

Nik continued to look somberly at the bridge. "It isn't just because I want my archivist back," he said.

Christine stopped before she picked up the next rock, puzzled. "Oh, oh!" she said. She hung her head. She'd forgotten that she was supposed to work at Nikolai's Magical Emporium the past weekend. She catalogued old books and organized all his supplies for him in exchange for the occasional magical lesson. "I'm sorry," Christine said.

"It's okay," Nik told her. "I understand you're rather involved with all this," he added, waving a hand at the

LEAH R CUTTER

partially assembled bridge. "Do you suppose you could come next weekend, then?" he asked.

Christine blinked, surprised. She'd thought that Nik let her work in the shop primarily because he thought of her as a charity case. She wasn't doing work that he couldn't get hundreds of others to do.

Was she?

"I will come by this Saturday," Christine said slowly. It was only Monday. She could still get in a lot of work between now and then.

Nik looked at her expectantly.

"I promise," Christine added. She'd been raised in a human family where it had always meant something to give your word. As troll royalty, making a promise meant even more.

"Thank you," Nik said. And his wooden face did bear an expression of gratitude. "But I think you should probably go home now. Rest. Tomorrow the stone work will flow," he prophesied.

"All right," Christine said. She didn't mean to sound as grudging as she probably did. She couldn't help but yawn. She'd been up early to work, then a quick supper, then here at the park, working through the cold night.

"Good night," Nik said. He stepped away and vanished.

Christine rolled her eyes. Showoff. She needed to find a portal to do that sort of thing, as did most of the *kith and kin*, the various races that included orcs, halflings, brownies, even the elves and fairies. A powerful human magician might be able to do what Nik had just done. Certainly the members of the Host, which was composed of both angels and demons, had that ability as well.

She stretched her back and found herself yawning. My, she was tired! Maybe she'd take half a sick day.

But she knew she wouldn't. She had an obligation to her employer that she couldn't just skip. An obligation to her family. And now, it seemed, yet one more obligation, to Nik, her…friend? Teacher? Magical mentor?

She was too tired to figure it all out. Hopefully Nik was right, and not only would the stone work flow, but the rest of her life as well.

Christine woke with a start. What was that? She blinked, trying to place herself. She was in her own bed, in her lovely basement apartment. The windows that ran high across the wall above her bed, close to the ceiling, were still dark. The room smelled of the peppermint tea she'd made herself before going to sleep. Heavy, warm blankets covered her, encouraging her to just go back to sleep.

What time was it? She groaned when she looked at the clock. 5:30 AM. She'd never get back to sleep before her alarm went off at 6.

The phone charging on the end table next to the bed chirped at her again.

Damn it! She had her phone set to do no disturb until 6 AM, with a few exceptions.

Like Tina, her human doppleganger.

Christine sighed and grabbed her phone, dragging it

over to her. Why was Tina texting her this early in the morning?

Call me first thing!

I have NEWS!

Christine shook her head. Had Tina found yet another "love of her life"? The previous one had lasted at least two weeks.

Well, since Tina appeared to be up, Christine may as well call her.

The phone gave half a ring before Tina's excited voice came on the line. "Hi! What are you doing up so early?"

"You texted me and woke me up," Christine grumbled.

"Oops! Sorry!" Tina said, though she didn't sound the least bit sorry.

"What's so important?" Christine asked. She couldn't help but yawn a bit.

"I started doing some research into changeling spells," Tina gushed. "And I realized pretty quickly that it's a specialized skill. There are entire branches of spells dedicated just to capturing and making troll changelings!"

"Of course there are," Christine said dryly. Humans seemed to love using troll babies for changelings. She still wasn't sure why. Did trolls just give up their babies that easily? Or were troll babies just the easiest of the *kith and kin* to kidnap?

"Anyway, I realized that there was no way my parents could have done the changeling spell themselves," Tina hurriedly said, as if she realized that she'd touched on a sore spot. "They must have hired someone."

That made Christine blink and push herself up to

sitting. "Interesting," she said. "Do you know who they hired?"

"I think so, yeah," Tina said. "I have this godmother, see. Mama Albina. She's a real hag. I could never figure out why my parents would have chosen her for my godmother. They didn't even seem to like each other very much. But she'd show up, like clockwork, for Fourth of July and Christmas, every year."

"And you think she's the one your parents hired to do the changeling spell?" Christine asked.

"I found a list of changeling specialists, and she's the highest rated in Seattle," Tina said. "And my parents would have only hired the best."

"Hmmm," Christine said, trying to wake up her brain enough to think. "Did you ask them who they'd hired?"

"They told me not to be so vulgar," Tina said, the anger evident in her voice.

"I'm sorry," Christine said, nodding in sympathy. "It sucks when you figure out your parents aren't the paragons you thought they were."

Though her own parents, the ones who'd raised her, had turned out to be pretty awesome when they'd discovered they'd raised a changeling and not a real human girl…

"Anyway, I wanted to know if you wanted to go talk with her tonight. See if we could find out more about the changeling spell, or if she suspected that there was something special about you," Tina said.

"Sure!" Christine said, though she knew that if she went out with Tina she wouldn't be able to work on the bridge that night. She had made such good progress Tuesday night, after Nik had helped her on Monday.

"I'll meet you at the library at five," Tina said. "Maybe we can try one of those restaurants you and Ty seem to favor."

"All right," Christine said, though she'd have to give it some thought. A lot of the places where Ty, the demon hunter, took Christine for lunch seemed to cater only to *kith and kin*. She wasn't sure how they'd react if she brought a human with her.

She gave an inaudible sigh. Why couldn't the races, the humans, the *kith and kin*, and the Host—mainly the angels and demons—all just get along? Though she supposed, given the very nature of demons and such, that they were predisposed not to.

"Great! I'll set our meeting up. See you tonight after work!" Tina said. "Bye."

"Bye," Christine said as she carefully swiped off her phone. It had taken a lot of effort to put a protection spell on the face of her phone so that she didn't accidentally scratch it with her claws. Even after she'd tinkered with it, the spell still wasn't that strong. She had to watch what she did.

Christine sat for a moment, pondering. Tina felt guilty about what had happened, even though the events had taken place right when she'd been born. Christine had been "stolen" from Trollville in order to save her life, though both her bio-dad and her uncle, the king, had believed she was dead. Christine's bio-mom had died sometime after she'd been taken.

Tina's parents, the Zimmermans, had obeyed the letter

of the law and formally adopted Christine. However, at least as far as she was concerned, they hadn't done the morally right thing. Instead of keeping Christine to raise as their own, they'd pawned her off on the Tuckermans as soon as they could, taking their human baby.

They'd justified their acts by claiming it was to protect Tina's Destiny. Which, since Christine had broken the changeling spell, had become muddled.

Did Tina still have a Destiny? Did Christine?

Did it matter? Oracles and their prophecies always seemed deliberately obscure.

So Tina was determined to help in any way she could, in particular by ferreting out as much information as she could about what had happened to Christine when she'd been made into a changeling. And Christine trusted her human doppelganger, even though she'd seen firsthand how easy it was for a demon to corrupt a human.

With a sigh, Christine flipped back her covers and slid out of bed, stretching. She'd taken a long hot soak in Epsom salts the night before, after working (successfully for once!) on the fairy bridge. As a troll, she healed remarkably fast.

However, she was still stiff. Since she was up so early, she could take another bath instead of having to shower.

Then she'd have to wear something that this Mama Albina would approve of.

Christine assumed that probably, no matter what she did, Mama Albina wouldn't actually like her.

No matter. Christine could now take care of herself, much better than ever before. Not just physically, with her regular fight training with Patrick the orc, but magically as well.

As Christine ran the water for her tub, she had a strange sense of vertigo, of standing on the edge of a cliff, about to race down.

Were things actually moving for her? Finally?

CHAPTER 2

C hristine waited for Tina just inside the lower door of the downtown Seattle library. Every time she had to wait upstairs made her grateful that she worked downstairs in the basement, in the archives. The building was a modern marvel of glass and round metal pipes. It was built on one of the steeper blocks, so the lower level was several stories below the upper street level.

While Christine was certain that Tina probably loved the upper levels, they always made Christine nervous. The space was so wide open and exposed. It was the opposite of everything that she liked: dark, enclosed, safe.

Tina had texted that she was stuck in traffic. That had surprised Christine—she'd expected Tina to just use a portal when she traveled anywhere in the city. Maybe, though, they would need to drive to see Mama Albina.

Christine recognized Tina just from her walk as she came up the sidewalk, her blonde head bobbing in time with her own sense of inner joy.

Christine would never admit to being envious of Tina's happiness. Christine still felt that she was learning how to be herself, as well as what she needed to do in order to be happy. The changeling spell had affected her entire life. It had made Christine afraid to try new things, to stand out or be noticed. It had even given her a slight sense of agoraphobia, making her feel as though once she got into her apartment at night, she could never go out again.

It was hard, sometimes, for Christine to figure out what were actually her own tastes and preferences. The changeling spell had ensured that Tina's likes and dislikes had imprinted on Christine, so until the spell had been broken, they'd had identical tastes in food, clothing, music, and most importantly, books.

Christine actually found it easier to figure out what *she* wanted when she was hanging out with Tina. When Tina expressed an opinion or preference, Christine often felt it either resonate within her, or occasionally repulse her, which told her what was her and what wasn't.

Tina smiled brightly when she saw Christine. Or rather, more brightly. People gravitated toward Tina, while they would avoid Christine, particularly if she was feeling "trollish" and grumbly.

Tina wore a fashionable black raincoat that came down to mid-thigh. She had it unzipped, showing the bright white lining around her face. She wore a nice-looking sea-green blouse, tucked into skinny jeans, showing off her tiny waist. Black ankle boots completed the look.

She could have been a model, particularly since she'd

inherited the porcelain, apples-and-cream skin that all the Tuckermans had.

Christine felt like a dark shadow in comparison. While her human appearance shared similar features to Tina's, they were all done darkly. Her human skin was dark and olive-toned. Instead of shiny, blond, smooth hair, Christine's was black and coarse. She stood at least a foot taller than Tina, with more curves as well.

Part of that was the law of conservation. While Christine was much larger in her natural troll state, she had to have enough muscle mass in her human state to support such a size.

"Hi there!" Tina said as she came up. She knew better than to give Christine a hug, though Christine could tell that Tina always wanted to.

Christine had never been comfortable with people touching her. A large part of that was due to her troll nature, though some of it she suspected was just her.

Still, Christine appreciated Tina's restraint, and so reached out and squeezed Tina's bicep. "Hi," Christine said, letting go quickly.

"So where are we going for dinner?" Tina asked as they waited for the light so they could cross Madison and continue heading south.

"Italian place just up the way," Christine said. She'd gone there with Ty a few months back, and she was certain that at least half the clientele had been human.

The chef on the other hand...

"It's a bit different than a regular restaurant," Christine warned.

"Duh," Tina said, rolling her eyes. "This is why I love

eating out with you! You know all the strange and exotic places."

Christine tried not to bristle. Just because she wasn't human didn't make her *exotic*. But she knew that Tina didn't mean anything by it. It was just how she'd been raised.

Tina chatted happily about her day and the spells she'd been working on. Christine let the conversation soothe her. She really did like hanging out with Tina. The topic changed to books, and of course they both had to gush about their latest read.

Christine's to-be-read pile was really getting out of hand, particularly since she was spending all her time working at the park, rebuilding the bridge.

But someday…Someday maybe she'd really be able to sit and read to her heart's content. If she could, she'd make sure that got added to the job description for princess.

The restaurant was located under the building, which made it more comfortable for Christine. About two dozen tables filled the space, each covered with a cheap vinyl red-and-white-checked tablecloth. The smell of garlic and tomato sauce engulfed Christine, making her mouth water.

A harried-looking waitress waved them toward one of the open tables at the back.

Tacky paintings of Elvis on rich black velvet hung on the walls, more than one as tall as Christine. Song scores with lyrics painted in glitter hung on some of the others. Christine didn't like looking at those for too long, or the tune would be stuck in her head for a week. A lone six-string guitar, signed by the King himself, stood in a place of honor in the corner, protected by a thick (and Christine suspected, bulletproof) clear plastic case.

Christine never looked too closely at that table either, as she suspected she'd find remnants of incense and other offerings being made to the King.

"You're right, this place has character," Tina said, gaping as she looked around.

Christine scanned the room. As before, the diners were half human and half not. At least Tina wouldn't get any guff here and no one would ask Christine if Tina was her pet.

"Uhmmm, where's the menu?" Tina asked after a moment. She flipped over the single small sheet that listed drinks, but no food.

"There isn't any," Christine said with a grin. "Just wait, you'll see," she counseled her friend.

After a short while, a tall, proud man came over to their table. He wasn't human, despite his appearance, but Christine had never pried or even tried to figure out exactly what race he was.

He had a tall forehead with receding white curls. A large nose jutted out from his flat face, below piercing blue eyes. His chin was also long and white stubble clung to it. Smile wrinkles curved around the edges of his pale lips and the corners of his eyes.

He wore a white chef's coat and pants, with the title "Chef Guido" stitched in red over his left breast pocket.

"Welcome, welcome!" he said in a booming voice. "How hungry are you ladies?"

Christine told him, "Hungry." And she was. She'd

eaten a lighter lunch because she knew they'd be coming here.

Tina shrugged. "So-so."

That didn't surprise Christine. Tina hadn't always enjoyed the food at the places Christine brought her to.

"Any allergies?" the chef asked.

"More meat and veggies, light on the pasta," Christine informed him. She'd found that once she'd become a troll, her palate had changed. No matter how fresh or artisanal the bread was, it all tasted like cardboard to her.

"No eggplant," Tina said.

Christine found herself nodding. Huh. She hadn't realized that she didn't like eggplant, not until Tina mentioned it.

"*Bueno!*" the chef said. "I bring you food soon."

He nodded and marched back to the kitchen.

"That's it?" Tina asked, her eyes wide. "That's brilliant!"

Christine grinned at her. It was sometimes so much fun to have a friend to explore things with!

Though at the same time, she still felt a pang: she wished she knew another troll that she could hang out with like this.

After dinner, they drove up north in Tina's car, all the way to Lynnwood, to get to Mama Albina's house.

Tina's parents had bought her the car. Tina had been surprised that Christine's parents hadn't done the same for her. Though Christine's family home was in a very rich neighborhood, her parents had only been able to afford it due to an inheritance.

"Aren't there any portals near here?" Christine asked as they drove up the uncrowded freeway. It surprised her that no one had built one. Particularly with the large stretches of trees interspersed with strip malls. Nice getaway from the city.

"There are," Tina said, "but they only go to the mall."

Figured. Even *kith and kin* liked to shop.

"Plus, Mama Albina has her entire subdivision very well protected. We couldn't pop in any closer than a mile or so," Tina warned.

Christine was impressed. Not many humans were that powerful. "You said Mama Albina was a hag," Christine said. She imagined an older woman who wore all black, with a huge hooked nose and warts. Maybe even sickly green skin.

"Just wait, you'll see," Tina teased.

Christine grinned. She'd used the same phrase on Tina earlier at the restaurant, and this was Tina's chance to tease her back. Dinner had been fabulous. Chef Guido had prepared the most delectable red meat sauce for Christine, served over zucchini noodles, while he'd made Tina a delicate lemon-alfredo sauce over butternut ravioli. They'd split a ginger panna cotta for dessert. Christine still felt full.

She glanced over at Tina, trying to read her mood. She seemed relaxed, content to drive, so Christine dared to ask, "Any word yet from the Oracles?"

Tina shrugged. Was she slightly more tense now? "The

readings are mixed," she said sourly. "One of the Oracles even proclaimed that I no longer have a Destiny! What is wrong with those people," she said crossly.

Christine wasn't sure if Tina was referring to the Oracles or to the driver who had nearly cut them off.

"They've just lost the thread. I still have a Destiny," Tina said after a bit.

Christine didn't know who Tina was trying to convince: Christine, or herself.

Tina turned off the highway and drove away from the mall, up the hill and into the middle of suburbia. The houses here were bigger, on larger plots of land, though some "McMansions" were tucked away in here as well, with the house taking up almost every square foot of space, people practically looking through each other's windows.

Christine shuddered. Though many would find her lovely "garden level" apartment uncomfortable, she adored it. She felt that the fact that it was mostly underground was one of its best features. It fit her just fine, though she still had daydreams about living in rock tunnels with gorgeous precious stones embedded in the walls.

Tina turned again, and again, winding her way through the quiet suburban streets with huge cars parked in the driveways, and no sidewalks.

Eventually, Tina drove into a cul-de-sac. At the apex of the circle squatted a huge house.

Christine nodded. While she couldn't imagine any sort of self-respecting hag living in such a clean neighborhood, the house more than made up for it. She half expected lightning to suddenly streak across the sky between the two front towers.

The streetlights barely lit the front yard, let alone the house. It loomed in the darkness. Christine felt as though many eyes peered out of the windows. She was certain the house was painted black or perhaps a midnight blue, with an equally dark roof, though she couldn't tell in the dim light. It had two towers in the front, not set at the corners or symmetrically. The one to her right was larger and taller and stood immediately to the side of the door. The one to her left was smaller, almost at the corner. They both had peaked, witchhat roofs.

No lights came on as they crossed the immaculately kept yard. The walk leading up from the street to the front door was also perfectly smooth concrete. No weeds would dare to peek out of the cracks there.

"Are you sure she's expecting us?" Christine asked quietly as they walked up to the dark doorway.

"I'm sure," Tina said as she rang the doorbell. "We wouldn't have been able to get this far if she hadn't wanted to see us."

"Oh," Christine said. This Mama Albina was really strong.

Then again, this was Mama Albina's home. Christine had learned that magic worked better when the magic caster had an affinity for the place.

Maybe that was why she'd been having so many problems with the bridge, since she'd never really felt comfortable there…

The door swung open silently. A tall white woman stood in front of them, thin as a rail, looking down her nose at them. She had perfectly styled hair pushed back from her forehead, ginger with gray streaks. Her eyes were a faded, watery blue, and gave a sense of great age. She wore a white-and-beige sweater set, with a matching knit skirt. Black-rimmed glasses hung around her neck on a gold and green chain.

Christine felt as though they were a second set of eyes staring at her with disapproval.

Power emanated from this woman, a solid wall of cool energy.

"So. You come. Both of you," Mama Albina said.

Christine stiffened but held her tongue. She didn't like the harsh tone in Mama Albina's voice at all.

"You can come in," Mama Albina said. "Wipe your feet," she instructed them. "No bring extra trash in."

Christine pushed her lips together. She was *not* about to rip Mama Albina a new one for that sort of treatment.

However, she might need a *long* workout at the gym after this meeting, so she could take out her aggression on a punching bag.

The entranceway looked charming enough. Dark wood wainscoting covered the lower half of the walls, with plain, cream-colored walls above. A spindly, antique table was pushed against the wall opposite the door, sporting pictures and knickknacks. Candles burned in wall sconces just above.

Christine and Tina both hung their coats on the wrought-iron coat tree standing to the left of the door. Just past that, a dark staircase went up. Christine shivered at the cold air that flowed down the stairs.

Mama Albina probably worked up there, in an eight-sided room with all the windows blacked over.

Tina led the way through the house. They walked past the staircase and a small alcove that held a table and large cupboards full of plates and bowls, past a partially closed door that led to a small toilet and sink, and into the kitchen.

Christine finally felt as though she could take a deep breath. The kitchen actually strove to be homey. Old-fashioned, black-and-white hexagon tiles made up the floor, held in place with black grout. The cupboards were all white painted wood, with black marble countertops. A red teapot bubbled on the white gas stove. Three cups had been set out, and the smell of lavender and vanilla filled the air.

Seemed they were going to have tea together.

Mama Albina sat on one side of her wooden kitchen table. Two empty chairs faced her. A folded-up newspaper lay pushed against the far end, next to the wall, along with a plain white salt and pepper shaker set.

That relieved Christine more than she could say. It made Mama Albina more human, with her morning paper and salted eggs.

"I expect you, Tina," Mama Albina said. "But I expect you alone. Why you bring *that* one?"

Deep breaths. Christine would *not* reach across the table and slap this woman.

At least, not until they'd learned more about what she knew.

"She's my sister," Tina said hotly. "No one else is as close to me."

"Good, good!" Mama Albina said, smiling. "The spell very strong, no? Her tastes, your tastes, same," she continued, finally addressing Christine. "You two even sit the same."

"Did it have to be that strong?" Christine asked, curious. No wonder Mama Albina didn't hold a high opinion of her! The old woman saw her as a poor imitation of Tina, nothing more.

"Ah, you have same smarts, too. Good," Mama Albina said. The kettle on the stove started whistling. Mama Albina pushed herself up. She shuffled over to make the tea.

Only then did Christine notice that Mama Albina wore big, soft, fuzzy slippers. They were completely at odds with the rest of her appearance. They made her much less scary.

Mama Albina came shuffling back to the table with the pot in one hand, the three mugs in the other. "To answer, no, spell not supposed to be that strong. Even for you, darling," she added, looking at Tina. "For your Destiny."

"Then why make it so strong?" Christine asked. It had always puzzled her that Tina's tastes had influenced her own so much.

Mama Albina sighed. She placed her hands on the table and glanced down at them. They looked like claws, and like her eyes, showed her true age. The skin was mottled with age spots. It had also worn so thin the blue veins showed starkly. Her hands couldn't straighten all the way, but remained slightly bent, like claws. The nails, of course, bore a perfect French manicure.

"I didn't make spell so strong," she admitted. "Not at first."

"What happened?" Tina asked when Mama Albina didn't continue.

A soft bell-like chime filled the room. Mama Albina picked up the white porcelain teapot and poured the golden liquid equally into the three cups.

"I am best at what I do," Mama Albina said softly. "No one better. Particularly with your kind," she added, nodding toward Christine.

Christine didn't bother trying to hide how she bristled. Mama Albina made it sound as though Christine and *her kind* were lower than the scum of the earth. Not intelligent enough to learn how to tie their own shoelaces.

"The spell, is usual, eh?" she continued, looking into the depths of her own tea mug as if maybe more answers lay there. "I have all ingredients laid out around the two cribs. Both babies asleep, though you fussed more," she said in an accusatory tone, glaring once at Christine.

Christine shrugged. She just figured her baby self had been smart enough to know trouble when she was in it.

"You had scars on your arms. Hell fire," Mama Albina said softly.

Christine gasped softly.

She'd believed Tina, that this had been the woman who'd performed the changeling spell. That Mama Albina remembered the scars on Christine's arms just reaffirmed it.

Tina didn't reach out to squeeze Christine's hand. She still bumped the back of her hand against the back of

Christine's where it lay on the table, a brief touch of warmth.

"I figured you in trouble. So I prepared everything. I start the binding." Mama Albina paused and looked off into the distance for a moment. "Spell is fine. Almost finished. Then…something enters the room."

The shiver that Mama Albina gave made Christine curious. This woman was a very strong, powerful witch. What would scare her?

"White light. So pure. But you are not human. An angel come to protect my girl?" Mama Albina asked, looking between the two of them.

"But the light no go to her. It goes to you," Mama Albina said, sounding accusatory. "Why? Why an angel there for you? Maybe it is demon light, hiding."

Christine found herself nodding. That made sense, actually. According to the old texts (and she still had to find the time to learn how to translate the originals, let alone teach herself to read old Trollish) the demons were set to watch over *kith and kin* while the angels were to look over humans.

"When I reach out, light repels me. Halfway across my room. *My* room," Mama Albina said.

Christine could tell that the powerful witch was still offended by that.

"Light arcs between one crib and the other. Then *poof,* gone, like never there," Mama Albina said. "I check the spell. Still strong as ever. I make it extra strong, then, to fight off whatever the white light does."

Christine found herself looking at Tina, who'd turned her head to look at Christine at the exact same moment.

"I had a Destiny," Tina said softly. "Do you think part of it got transferred to you?"

Christine shrugged. "Ming said that the only ones he'd bound powers of were those who would be powerful fighters or leaders in the Great War." She might have had her own Destiny, one that Ming had taken from her when he'd taken her powers.

Christine turned to look at Mama Albina. "Did I have my powers when you did the spell?" she asked.

"Powers? No. I cannot bind one with powers. Changeling spell wouldn't take." She paused, peering closely at Christine. "You have magic," she said. She sounded angry. "Show me. Your true face. Now."

Christine glanced at Tina, who just shrugged.

At least Christine had frequently practiced the main illusion spell that made her appear human, both putting it on as well as taking it off. She no longer had to shake herself like a wet dog.

Instead, Christine reached up and touched the necklace she always wore. At one point, it had held an illusion charm, until she'd burned it out. It was made out of silver metal, a looping design, with a rounded piece of blue glass just off the center of it.

Christine had originally been drawn to the asymmetry of the necklace. The troll royal sigil was asymmetric as well. Did that mean anything?

Just by touching the necklace and taking a deep breath, Christine was able to release her illusion spell. She "bulked out" instantly, feeling as though she suddenly took up twice as much space in the tiny kitchen.

She didn't add the illusion of a silver and gold tiara to

her hair, though she wanted to. She'd played around with various styles until she'd found the perfect one. She assumed her ivory tusks gleamed in the low lights of the kitchen. Her skin looked darker, less green. She pushed up the sleeves of her blouse, showing Mama Albina the scars that remained from the Hell fire.

Suddenly, Christine felt the presence of all of her internal powers. They sat perched, ready to attack. She swelled up even more, looming over the others though she still sat.

After studying Christine closely for a few long moments, Mama Albina sat back and nodded. "I did not know," she said slowly. "Your powers long gone before you came to me."

Christine knew that she had no reason to trust this Mama Albina. Nik had warned her again and again to never trust a human. And Christine had an inkling why he felt that way, particularly given how much influence the demons had over humans.

Still, Christine believed Mama Albina's story, that Christine hadn't had any powers. She'd been just another troll baby, there to be used to further the human agenda in the Great War that threatened.

"After that, I make your parents make me godmother. So I can see you. Check up on spell. It never unraveled," she said proudly. "Not until you broke it," she added with another glare at Christine.

All Christine could do was shrug. She couldn't be sorry that she'd done that, not in the least.

Mama Albina continued to scowl at Christine. "Now, her Destiny muddled. All because of you."

"Maybe her Destiny was to hide me," Christine couldn't help but say.

"Only humans have Destiny," Mama Albina said, sitting up stiffly.

Tina gasped quietly. "The Oracles—they only predict human Destinies," she said. "But you had a Destiny too, didn't you? That Ming muddled when he took away your powers."

"Do you think we could go visit the Oracles? And the non-human ones as well?" Christine asked.

"Road trip!" Tina said joyfully.

"Bah," Mama Albina said. "Destinies. I see them come. I see them go. You both be careful when listening to Oracles, careful what you believe. Yes?"

Both Christine and Tina nodded solemnly.

Christine already knew to not trust humans, particularly not ones called Oracles.

But where was she going to find the Oracles for her kind?

CHAPTER 3

Christine slid yet another stone into place. It joined its neighbors with a satisfying *click*. It made her want to howl with joy when she took a step back and saw the progress she'd made, after just two nights of work! She'd just needed to listen more to how the stones went together. She'd figured out how her earth power could help her determine how the broken rocks fit, soothing them as she slipped them together.

The Zimmermans had wanted to force the bridge into being, to dominate the rocks and stones, to bend them to their will.

Christine now realized just how far the Zimmermans had led her down the wrong path. She didn't think they'd done it on purpose. It was just how they were.

How humans were, come to think of it.

Maybe artists respected their materials more, and worked more with what was there. Christine knew she'd read that someplace, about a sculptor finding the figure existing already in the marble.

In the meantime, it was so nice to work *with* the rock, instead of having it always fight her. She wouldn't say that the stones cooperated, not quite. But they were more sluggish now, passively resisting her, rather than being actively opposed to being joined together.

She stepped back, pleased with her work. She could actually *see* the progress she'd made, the gap between the two halves of the bridge noticeably smaller.

She would have to be sure to thank Nik again for his help. And to see if he'd give her any other hints or tips. Nik was notoriously close-mouthed about such things, only saying something when he was one hundred percent certain.

Christine didn't know why the wooden shopkeeper was so cautious. It might have been because he was so old. He'd made references to being around during the last Great War, the one between the humans, the Host, and *kith and kin*. The humans had won that round. As a result, they'd been in dominance over the earth ever since.

The only problem was that the last Great War had been nearly two thousand years ago. Christine would never actually speculate out loud about what had really gone on back then, but part of her wondered how Jesus fit into the history of the war, and if he'd been part of the reason why the humans had won.

Finished for the day, Christine turned to go. She felt her exhaustion now, and she shivered in the night. It had grown colder than she'd realized. She glanced around. The park was deserted. She only heard the occasional swish of cars along Madison. (She still felt it was a failing of her race that her ears couldn't swivel like a dog's. She'd not been able to make them move on their own either, though she'd spent an entire afternoon, staring in a mirror, trying to get them to, at the very least, twitch.)

How late was it? She pulled her phone out, then groaned. Not only was it almost 11:30, she'd missed a call from Ty, the demon hunter. But fortunately, he'd left a voicemail.

If anyone would be able to find an Oracle who predicted the futures of *kith and kin*, Ty could.

"Hey there," Ty's friendly voice came over the line.

If only Ty were a troll, and not just *kith and kin*… Christine sighed. Though she adored Ty, she never would have tried to move beyond the friendship zone with him. Only other trolls interested her that way.

"I have good news and bad news," he had recorded. "Want to do lunch tomorrow? Text me."

That made Christine grin. *Ty for lunch* had been a running joke between them for over half a year, now.

She texted him, let him know that she was game, then hurried out of the park. While it was good that the rain had stopped, it also meant the temperature had dropped considerably.

Hopefully the next time it started to rain it wouldn't come down as snow…

Christine hopped on the last bus up the hill. She knew she was a mess. She didn't care.

She nearly reached over and rang the bell to get off on the next stop when she saw who else was in there.

The last row of seats across the back of the bus was filled with scruffy demons, at least eight of them. They had a hyena look to their long snouts and feral eyes. Christine

37

didn't bother trying to see how they presented as humans, though she suspected they'd look like street kids.

However, it was too late. They'd caught her scent. If she left now, they'd merely chase after her.

She'd seen more demons in Seattle lately. It worried her. Were the demons gathering as part of the Great War? Were they planning to attack not just pocket worlds but human cities as well?

Christine chose a seat close to the rear exit, so she could escape quickly if it came to that. Not because she couldn't defend herself, but she didn't want any human collateral. She ignored the raucous laughter spiking behind her. She also didn't bother listening to their snorting noises, and assumed they were talking to someone else when they called, "Here piggy, piggy!"

Christine pulled out her phone to text her brother, Dennis. Chances were that he was asleep and wouldn't want to talk with her. There was also a slim chance that he was up, and nearby. He frequently went to bars on Capitol Hill with his friends, even on weeknights.

You still "born ready"?

Though Dennis was merely human, the idiots sitting behind her had no true bravery or courage. They'd flee soon enough. Plus, Christine felt certain that she'd be able to protect her baby brother, while at the same time, give him a thrill.

It wasn't like she was itching for a fight or something. No, really. As a troll, she wouldn't fight anyone unless they threw the first punch. No one had had to teach her that. It was an instinct.

She'd bet the stupid pack sitting behind her didn't know that about trolls.

And quite frankly, if they attacked Dennis, that was as good as throwing the first punch as far as she was concerned.

Of course! Where and when?

Christine couldn't help but grin. Only her brother.

Though it was sometimes rough being a troll in a human family, they still worked to accept her regardless, trying to make her still feel like she was, well, family.

The bus would let her out four long blocks from her cozy apartment. The punks would follow her, harassing her. She could put on a show of being scared.

She sent Dennis the intersection two blocks away from her place, and a time of fifteen minutes.

His response?

Be there in five

Christine grinned. This was going to be so much fun.

Of course, no plan survived contact with the enemy. Christine had read that, but she'd thought this time, things would be different.

The pack of demons had followed her off the bus, as she'd known they would. They came sniffing along behind her, still making snorting noises and pig jokes.

However, she'd only gotten a block off of the main drag before they'd attacked, not two blocks, so Christine was still by herself. The only warning Christine had was the sound of their boots hitting the pavement too near to her.

Christine slashed out with claws at the ready. But she sliced through empty air as she pivoted. The pack melted around her, surrounding her. The smell of them hit her, making her gag: like roadkill that had been baking in the hot sun. She whirled around, trying to keep them in front of her, but there were too many of them.

Only after she missed clawing through the next one did she realize that something was wrong.

They weren't as solid as they should be.

Damn it. They were shadow demons. They only halfway existed in this plane.

Fortunately, all of Christine's power elements rose up, ready to help her fight. She blasted the two in front of her with a great gout of fire. It was generally her best defense. Most creatures were vulnerable to fire.

However, that just made the pair of them giggle as they danced away.

They were too much a mix of this plane and that. Regular fire wouldn't affect them. Hell fire would, but Christine hadn't tried to learn how to do that. She wasn't sure if she could, and she was afraid of what it would say about her if the ability came easy.

Her air element tried next, flinging out a freezing web of air that tangled up two of the creatures.

They only stayed frozen for a short time, though. They were able to crack themselves out of it, the shards of ice tinkling off the hard concrete.

One of the demons tried to grab Christine's arm.

However, that meant that it had to make itself solid enough to touch her.

Big mistake.

Christine grabbed hold of the little demon and punched it soundly in the snout. Its head snapped back and Christine punched it a second time, a little harder, its teeth grazing the back of her hand. Then she dropped him. He lay where he fell.

Christine let out a loud growl that echoed menacingly up and down the street.

At least the shadow demons learned from their fallen partner's mistake. None of the others tried to grab her.

That didn't stop the attack. They circled her, whining and panting like hungry dogs.

The next attack came from behind, a long ripping sound echoing in the night.

Damn it! She really liked this jacket. But it was destroyed now.

The way her skin burned told her that the claws were probably poisonous. Fortunately, that wouldn't bother her —her troll metabolism would heal despite them.

Christine heard her brother's footsteps come running up the sidewalk. The pack turned to look at him.

This wasn't good.

She'd gotten cocky. Now, a human was involved.

"Run away," Christine told Dennis.

"Nuh-uh," Dennis said, blinking as though he couldn't quite see what the threat was.

Christine conjured a string of lights, jewel-colored and each about the size of her fist, then sent it dancing around Dennis, lighting his way and hopefully confusing the shadow demons enough that they wouldn't try to hurt him.

Then she studied the pack as they shifted and moved. That one. The tallest of them, with the chest the most puffed out. He had to be the leader.

Take him out, and the rest would fall back, like cutting the head off a snake.

She took a deep breath, then reached out with both her hands, fingers spread wide. She rotated her wrists until they touched, then she forced a deep gout of power through her hands.

It was unfocused. But she didn't know what else to do. She had to get out of there, with Dennis. Now.

The power blasted out in a great white cone. It froze the head demon. The half of his face that Christine could see showed tremendous shock.

Then Christine twisted the power. Added in a touch of water and ice.

The leader stayed where he was. Christine would have dropped rocks on him next, if she could have found them quickly enough.

Instead, two members of the pack suddenly raced at their leader. They ran low, like they were coming to tackle him.

It surprised Christine that they actually did tackle him, forcing him to the ground.

Out of reach of her cone.

She tried to adjust it, to aim it down at the three of them, but she didn't have enough control.

Still, it didn't seem to matter. The pack raced off, howling and gibbering.

Christine turned toward Dennis. The string of lights still surrounded him, circling his torso three times. It hadn't completely stopped the demons: one had gotten in a good swipe at Dennis' right arm. The jacket was shredded and Christine could smell the blood.

"Oh, Dennis, I'm so sorry," she said, rushing up to him.

He gave her the biggest grin. "I wouldn't have missed that for anything! Did you see how they ran?"

"I still shouldn't have brought you here," Christine said, reaching out for the lights.

"Yes, you should have," Dennis said. "While you were focused on the big guy, I kept three of the others distracted so they wouldn't attack you."

When the lights disappeared, Dennis suddenly swayed. "I…I don't feel so good," he said.

Crap. She bet Dennis had been poisoned.

Christine took a critical look at Dennis' arm.

"How do you feel about the ER?" she asked, nervous.

"You know, I think that might be a good idea," Dennis said. "Before I pass out."

Christine caught her brother, lifting him easily.

"Hey, hey!" he said. "Put me down."

"Nope," Christine said. "This is to make up for the time I set fire to your car."

"How is this making that up to me?" Dennis demanded. He suddenly sounded stronger and more clear-headed than he had. Probably because he was pissed off.

"By saving your life, idiot," Christine told him.

"I—"

"Shush," Christine said. She hurried back a block, then raced halfway up the hill and down an alley.

"We aren't going the right direction, you know," Dennis commented dryly. "The emergency room is that way," he said, waving a hand behind him.

"I know," Christine said. This house? No. The next. It had a Japanese-style gate at the back, leading from the alley into the backyard. When the people had left for vacation once, they'd placed a Buddha in the center of the doorway, as if to warn people away.

"Do we know these people?" Dennis asked. "Can they help?"

"No," Christine said. She suspected the humans in the house had no idea what their back gate represented. "But this is the quickest way. Trust me."

Dennis nodded, dropping his head against her shoulder.

He didn't say anything else.

Christine shrugged Dennis back further in her arms, then used small, awkward movements with her hands to form a portal. A faint shimmer coated the unpainted wooden gate. Keeping the image of the entrance to emergency care firmly in her mind, Christine stepped through.

Fortunately, no one was on the other side to see her step out of thin air. Then again, most of the time when humans saw something that was clearly impossible, their brains explained it away, giving them the most plausible reasons.

Dennis looked bad. Sweat stood out on his pale

forehead and his jaw was slack. He was still breathing, though.

"Help me!" Christine called as she passed through the doors. "My brother's been stabbed."

Instantly three people rushed toward her, helping her lay Dennis down on a cart. "I think the blade was poisoned," Christine added.

She held his hand as he was wheeled back, a nurse with a clipboard following her. Christine fished Dennis' wallet out of his jeans pocket and was able to give the hospital his insurance information.

Fortunately, her own back was already healing, and she brushed aside all of the staff's concerns about her.

The doctor who came out to greet them looked like he was twelve, at most. He was Indian, with black hair and big black eyes. He barely came up to Christine's chest, and his fingers looked like long bones in the purple gloves he wore.

"This looks bad," he said, peeling back the edges of Dennis' shirt with tweezers. "What happened?"

Christine sighed and explained how they were attacked by a group of street kids who'd followed her home from her bus stop. She explained that everything had happened so fast (and it had) and that the blade had been tipped in something black and dripping (it hadn't, and it hadn't been a blade, but that was the best that she could come up with at the time).

"Some sort of acid, perhaps?" the doctor asked, peering closely at the wound.

Christine could only nod. She couldn't explain that

her brother was possibly infected with shadows. She wasn't even sure if that was possible.

Maybe she should have taken him to a clinic for *kith and kin*, though she wasn't sure that such a thing existed. She was going to have to ask Patrick the next time she saw him at the gym.

"Is your brother allergic to any medications? Any history of heart attack or stroke? Diabetes? Cancer?" The doctor ran through the list at breakneck speed. "We will irrigate the wound first, see if that will clear out most of the poison, as well as start him on antibiotics."

Why would they treat poison with antibiotics? Christine was going to have to look that one up.

The doctor and nurses stripped Dennis' shirt off and began treating his arm. It looked like it hurt. A lot.

However, as soon as the skin was cleaned off, the blackness stopped spreading. After they sprayed his arm with some sort of solvent, the wound appeared to shrink back in on itself.

Christine was still worried that the darkness had already sunk into her brother's veins.

How was she going to fix this?

Christine waited in the curtained-off room, watching Dennis breathe. The machines beside him beeped with his heart. A blood pressure cuff hissed to life now and again. At least the numbers stayed steady.

The room stank of industrial cleaners. The smell made her want to sneeze. The temperature was cool enough that

Christine kept her ruined jacket on over her shoulders. Ghastly posters showing the insides of eyes as well as the cardiovascular system of humans lined the walls where there weren't cupboards and more supplies.

Dennis appeared to be getting better. Christine had called Mum and Dad and had explained the situation. She also requested that they stay home until they at least had found out which hospital room Dennis had been assigned to. The doctors thought he was in the clear, but they wanted to keep him overnight for observation.

Finally, Dennis blinked, then blinked again. He opened his eyes and looked around. Christine immediately leaped out of the uncomfortable plastic hospital chair to stand beside him.

"Hospital?" Dennis asked. He still looked far too pale lying on the hospital bed, with the white-and-green-striped hospital gown tied high around his neck.

"Yes," Christine said. "They want to keep you here overnight for observation."

She looked closely at her brother when she said that. She couldn't see any magic in or around the bandaged wound. She should have gone and fetched some holy water to clean it. Maybe she should stock some of that at her apartment, just in case.

"We sure showed them, eh?" Dennis said.

Christine rolled her eyes. "Yes, we did," she said. "I'm sorry you got hurt," she added.

"It was an adventure," Dennis said. He tried to sit up.

Christine helped him up, then raised the back of the bed to support him.

"You know, you're my sister and I love you and all,"

Dennis said, looking around. "But, ah, does that door in the corner lead to a bathroom? Could you get them to unhook me so I could use it? Or do I need a bedpan?"

Christine reached over and pressed the nurse call button. "I'm sure you'll be fine," she said. She couldn't express the relief she felt, seeing Dennis feeling so much better.

But she couldn't kill that niggling doubt that he might still be sick.

CHAPTER 4

After staying up with Dennis until after 2 AM, Christine called in sick the next day for work. It was Friday, and she just planned on taking a long weekend. Sleep late, go have lunch with Ty, then spend the entire afternoon working on the bridge.

If she could just put in enough time this weekend, she might actually be able to finish it…

And then what? Christine knew she had to travel to Trollville, to get her bio-dad out of prison. Hell, maybe even see what it was like to be a princess.

But what would she do after that? She didn't know if she'd want to stay in Trollville, or if she'd always feel drawn back to the human plane. If princesses did good works, like human royalty seemed to be so fond of, then one of her main causes would be to stop the trafficking of troll babies.

Christine dressed warmly, as the weather had cooled again. No clouds marred the bright blue sky. She thought it was unfair. It sure looked warmer than it was. She wore her cute new boots that were waterproof as well as fur lined, along with a heavy red-wool jacket that Mum had bought her for Christmas. She was going to have to replace her rain jacket. She sighed, wondering how she was going to manage yet *another* expense.

Ty stood waiting on the corner of Broadway and Olive, outside of the drugstore that had once been a theatre and still had the huge marquee out front, though now it advertised flu shots. He looked the same as always, a lanky African-American man with kind brown eyes and a long face. He was dressed warmly, in a navy-blue down jacket that made his muscled chest seem even broader. He wore his usual jeans and heavy motorcycle boots, as well as a brown leather cap that looked like the kind that train conductors wore.

"Christine! Good to see you!" he said, stepping forward. He knew better than to hug her. He still smiled at her, then sniffed.

She always wondered how good his nose was and what he could tell about her. She knew that her own senses had grown much more acute once she'd broken the changeling spell.

"You hungry?" he asked as he turned and started walking up the street.

"Starved," she admitted. She'd slept through her alarm after her late night with Dennis. She'd only had enough time to shower and walk up to meet Ty. Street kids sat near the edge of the sidewalk, begging for money. Christine found herself edging closer to Ty as they passed them.

"What's up?" he asked quietly.

Christine sighed and told him of the attack the previous night. "I grew cocky," she said. "I shouldn't have asked Dennis to come along."

"But it sounds like you needed his help as well, if there were eight of them," Ty pointed out.

He turned and went down a small alley that Christine wasn't sure she'd seen before. Skylights above the arcade made the place seem too airy and bright. It wasn't like a nice dark alley at all. Clean wooden steps led up to the third floor. Ty took Christine down a small hallway to a blank door.

As he pushed the door open, the smell of roasted meat and sauerkraut floated out.

Christine's stomach rumbled in response.

The restaurant was as small as the Japanese restaurant he'd taken her to the previous month. There was a counter at the back with six chairs seated before it, all taken. The rest of the space was filled with a single huge long table. Everyone else seemed to be eating there, the food served family style. The people at the table passed around a huge basket of bread (ugh), along with large bowls of potatoes, meat, gravy, beets, sauerkraut, and other dishes Christine couldn't identify immediately.

Christine was surprised that Ty had brought her to such a crowded place. There was nowhere for them to sit and privately talk. Especially since Ty had said he had both good and bad news.

"Ty. Ty!" A heavy set Russian woman called to him from behind the counter. She was about as big around as Christine, barrel-chested, though with much larger breasts. A white kerchief tied at the corners lay on top of her light brown hair. She wore a bleached peasant shirt with red embroidery around the collar and cuffs, as well as a long blue-and-white-checked gingham apron.

It took Christine a moment to realize she wasn't human, but instead was *kith and kin*. Not troll, but something close. Orc, perhaps?

"Karina!" Ty called out in response, sounding happy.

Christine followed in his wake, pushing past the people already eating. Maybe they could eat first, talk later?

Karina kissed Ty on both cheeks before holding her arms out for Christine.

Christine forced herself to keep a smile on her face and allowed Karina to give her the same treatment.

"Come, come! I have table for you," Karina said. She turned to her right and pulled back a heavy, black velvet curtain.

As Christine walked past the curtain, the noise level abruptly dropped. She found her shoulders relaxing. It had been much louder than she'd realized in that other room.

This room was about the same size as the other. However, it held half a dozen tables, each curtained off from one other along three of the walls. Candles on the tables lit the area. Christine was glad she could see pretty well in the dark and wouldn't stumble.

"Thanks," Ty said as Karina showed them to their table.

Christine noted that all of the other beings back here weren't human. She asked Ty as she slid into her thickly padded chair, "The food here's that good?"

Ty beamed at her. "The best."

She also suspected that the way sound barely traveled through the air that spells and hidden charms were at work, making this a very private place to lunch.

"Despite the wonderful food, I don't come here often," Ty admitted. "I found Karina's son when he'd gone missing. She won't let me pay for a meal, now."

Christine nodded and didn't say anything. She'd seen the same behavior more than once at the various places Ty took her to, when Ty had helped someone out.

The menu was in several different languages. Christine grew excited when she realized that one of them was Trollish. However, she struggled to make out the words.

She'd never been good with languages. It was yet another reason why she wondered how she'd get along in Trollville. The king might not want an heir who didn't speak the same language he did.

She settled on the lamb meatballs over zucchini "noodles". That was one of the other things that she appreciated about the *kith and kin* restaurants: they generally catered to a meat and veggies crowd. She bet no bread would be served back here.

"So what's your news?" Christine asked after Karina had taken their orders.

"I think I found you an Oracle," Ty said.

When he didn't say anything more, Christine asked, "Is that the good news or the bad?"

"Both," Ty admitted. "The problem is that Oracles tend to be very race specific. So demons will only prophesize about demon Destinies, trolls will only prophesize about troll Destinies, and so on. There are no 'all purpose' Oracles, and only a few who dabble in cross-race futures."

Christine nodded. That kind of made sense. But it also didn't. Weren't the fates of all the races intertwined?

"So I figured since you and Tina probably have crossing fates, that you needed to find an Oracle who specialized in that sort of thing," Ty said.

"What's the problem?" Christine asked.

"He's human," Ty said. Though Ty didn't hold all humans in disregard, he still trusted *kith and kin* more. "And he's a performer."

"So take everything he says with a mountain of salt?" Christine asked.

Ty shook his head. He pressed his lips together as if he didn't want to say anything more.

"Is it not safe to go see him?" she asked quietly.

Ty finally gave her a smile again. "Oh, no, darling, I think you'd be safe. And your doppelganger. This Lunar Honeycomb much prefers the company of men to women."

Christine shrugged. She'd been raised in Seattle, and lived on Capitol Hill, where she frequently saw men holding hands, as well as women. To say nothing of annual events, such as Pride weekend or even the dykes versus drag queens baseball game. "And?" she prompted Ty.

"There's something about him," Ty said slowly. "Something slippery. He doesn't have magic. But he has… something. You be careful around him. Very careful. All right?"

"Message received loud and clear," Christine said. She

still felt guilty about getting Dennis injured the night before. She would not get cocky again.

After Karina delivered their drinks, Christine said, "Can I ask a favor? Do you think you could come over for Sunday dinner this weekend? To see if you can find any scent of shadow or poison or something else in Dennis?"

"I'd be delighted to," Ty said. "Your mum knows her way around a shepherd's pie."

"That she does," Christine said, making a mental note to ask Mum to make that for dinner.

"Should I take Tina with me to visit this Lunar Honeycomb?" Christine asked as their meals were being delivered. Though she knew that Tina could take care of herself, Christine still thought of herself as much tougher.

"Normally, I'd say you should go alone, but I think in this case, you both need to go," Ty said. He sighed. "Make sure you have extra protection spells with you. And maybe a good sharp knife. Just in case."

Christine nodded. She knew that Ty wasn't as worried about Christine facing an unknown opponent as he was Tina. Especially since Tina had been corrupted by demons, influenced by them, so much so that she'd attacked Christine instead of their common enemy.

Could this Lunar Honeycomb turn Tina's head the same way?

Christine didn't know. But she would be prepared, just in case.

~

"Hey, Mum," Christine said when her mother picked up the phone.

"Hello, darling," Mum said. "Is everything all right?"

Christine rolled her eyes. It was true that she rarely called anyone. She preferred texting to talking. However, she had been making more of an effort since she'd broken the changeling spell. It seemed that her parents needed reassurance that she was still their daughter despite not being quite human.

"Everything's fine, Mum," Christine said. She looked up the street again. No bus in sight. The bus app on her phone had told her that it would be a few minutes before the next one came. She stood alone on the corner, though a steady stream of people passed by, walking down the hill, on their way to work or school or wherever they were going.

The sky had stayed clear while Christine had had lunch with Ty. After she'd gone back home and changed into work clothes, clouds had started to blow in. Cold winds whipped around her. She still felt full and satisfied from lunch, but maybe she'd have to go get a cup of hot chocolate from one of the coffee shops close to the park.

"I, ah, have a favor to ask," Christine said as her mum waited. That was something else Christine appreciated about her family—they generally let her set the pace when it came to conversations. "Can I bring Ty to dinner on Sunday?"

"Certainly, darling! That would be lovely," Mum said warmly. "I'll make his favorite shepherd's pie. Oh, and you should bring Tina along as well. Lovely girl."

"Sure," Christine said. She knew her parents had mixed feeling about her human doppelganger. Tina was their natural child, their actual bio-daughter, but they hadn't raised her. She looked like them, but she wasn't family, not like Christine.

It got awkward sometimes.

"And I think that you should be your natural self at dinner, too," Mum added.

Christine muffled her groan. She knew it was just Mum making an effort to accept her troll daughter. However, it made things weird when Christine showed up in "troll face" as it were.

"Really? Are you sure you want me to be like that?" Christine asked, uncomfortable.

"Yes. Really," Mum said. "And Ty as well, if he wants to."

Christine shrugged. She'd text him later about it, stressing that it would be totally optional.

For him.

"All right, Mum, here's my bus," Christine lied.

"Oh! Are you off to work on the bridge?" Mum asked cheerfully. "How's it going?"

"It's going really well, finally," Christine said. She hesitated before she added, "I, ah, actually might be able to finish it at some point soon." She didn't want to give a date or a deadline. She'd made too much forward progress, followed by backwards progress over the months.

"Be sure to take some pictures before you leave," Mum said. She sounded excited.

"Will do. Bye!"

"Goodbye, dear," Mum said.

Did Mum not understand that when Christine finished the bridge that she'd be leaving? Going to Trollville? Or did Mum assume that Christine wouldn't stay there?

The bus appeared at the foot of the hill. Christine waited patiently as it made its way up, but she still had no answers.

∿

Christine put down the big rock she'd been holding when she heard the ringtone she'd assigned to Tina's number.

"Hey!" Christine said.

"Hey!" Tina said in return.

It sometimes weirded Christine out, how much Tina sounded like her.

"I'd love to go see this Lunar Honeycomb," Tina said immediately. "I looked up his performance times. He'll be at the Crescent Theatre tonight. Want to do dinner and a show?"

Christine winced. She couldn't afford the tickets, not really. "Won't he be too busy to see us, then? I mean, getting ready to perform and all?"

"Huh. I hadn't thought of that," Tina said.

Christine contained her sigh. Tina had been raised with so much privilege. She always assumed that everyone would accommodate her wishes and needs.

"Hold on," Tina said. "Okay. On his website, you can also schedule a psychic reading. His next open slot is...an hour from now. Otherwise, he's not available until next week."

Christine nodded. Of course she wasn't going to be able to get any more work done. Something always came up.

But it was important to get all this Destiny stuff figured out.

"I'm at the park," Christine said as she turned and started walking away. She was so close to being finished! There was only about a foot left before the edges of the bridge would touch each other again. She could sense the magic in the stones, tentatively reaching for each other. She figured the magic would be much stronger when she finished. "I need to go home and shower," Christine added.

"I'll meet you there in thirty," Tina said. "Bye!"

Christine couldn't begrudge her human twin her cheery nature. Tina was always bubbly that way.

Still, that didn't mean it didn't rankle Christine's trollish soul sometimes.

Christine waited outside her apartment. She'd showered and changed in record time. Clouds now filled the sky, and the weather reports predicted snow. She wore her bright red-wool jacket, along with her warmest boots. She didn't get as cold as she used to, now that she was fully a troll. Still, she didn't like snow.

Would Tina come and get her in her car? Or were they taking a portal? Christine assumed car, as they'd need thirty minutes to drive out to the theater, up along Rainier Avenue.

Tina's car came driving by slowly. Christine walked out to the street and hopped in. "Hi!" she said. The car smelled of Tina's lavender shampoo and the expensive leather seats. Tina wore a black leather coat from an Italian designer. Christine knew the coat was butter-soft and the leather easily damaged.

"Do you know why Ty warned you about this Lunar Honeycomb character?" Tina asked as she pulled forward.

Christine wasn't about to admit that Ty had been more worried about Tina than Christine. "Nope," she said. "Just that we needed to be extra careful."

"In my bag," Tina said, pointing to the large black purse sitting at Christine's feet, "you'll find a couple of protection charms."

Christine shook her head but dutifully pulled up Tina's bag. How could Tina be so free? How could she just hand Christine her bag (or her phone!) and invite Christine to use it? Christine didn't get it. It wasn't as if she had anything to hide in the little gray purse that she always carried, however, she wasn't sure she trusted anyone enough to just hand it to them.

Maybe she'd try, someday, if she ever found a troll boyfriend…

Christine pulled out a smooth silk pouch from a side pocket of Tina's bag. The color reminded her of gold and riches beyond belief. She rubbed her fingers across it carefully, then closed her eyes, focusing on what she felt and sensed.

Two spots of magic danced under her fingertips. They

both felt flat and roundish, like coins. Their magic felt contained, unable to spread. The smell of sweet jasmine filled her nose, tinged with soap. Something astringent, to keep them clean, perhaps?

Christine held up the bag for Tina to see.

"Yup. That's it. Don't take them out of the bag," Tina warned.

Christine nodded. That was what she'd expected. The bag contained the charms, stopped them from fully activating.

"When we get to the theatre, we each have one. I'd suggest putting it in your pocket or something. It won't last for very long," Tina said.

"Hopefully we won't need them at all," Christine said.

However, given how spooked Ty had been…

"I went and watched one of Lunar Honeycomb's YouTube videos," Tina said.

"What does he do? What's his performance like?" Christine asked, curious. She'd wanted to do so as well, once Ty had told her about him. However, she hadn't had a good enough connection while on her phone to watch one yet.

"Uhmmm, it's different. He's a tall white bald guy. With a huge black mustache curled up on the ends," Tina said. "And he's hairy. All over. In the video, he wore a gorgeous red satin dress, fully padded. Even though his chest hairs still stuck out over the top of it."

Christine nodded, trying to visualize it. Big boobs with lots of black chest hair. Cinched waist and big curvy hips.

It didn't do anything for her, but she was sure that someone would be turned on by it.

Then again, she was attracted to green skin and troll fangs.

"So what did he do in his performance?" Christine asked when Tina didn't say anything more.

"He also wore white satin gloves, that went up to his elbows," Tina said. "He had this glass ball that he passed back and forth between his hands while he did a lip synch. It was mesmerizing. It wasn't magic, I would swear by that, but the ball traveled so smoothly from one hand, up his arm, then back down again to the other. Like it was on a track or something."

"Okay," Christine said slowly. It sounded weird. "Will these charms protect us against being mesmerized?" Christine asked after a bit, still trying to imagine what Tina had seen. She was going to have to go look herself.

Tina nodded. "That was part of the reason why I watched a video first, before I called you. So I would know what kind of charms to buy."

To *buy*, not *make*. Christine couldn't contain her sigh. She would never be able to afford to just go out and buy a charm. She bet Tina had merely ordered it online, and Nik had sent it via portal express, so the charms had just shown up at her doorstep.

Christine didn't say anything though. Tina was funny about having her privilege pointed out to her. She'd argue that her life also had difficulties, particularly since she was figuring out that she preferred women to men.

"Thank you for getting the charms," Christine finally said. She knew that she was lucky that Tina had that kind of money and was very easy with it, always glad to share. If Christine ever decided she wanted to buy a house, or even a car, she knew that Tina would be happy to loan her the down payment.

"We'll watch each other's backs," Tina said. She glanced over at Christine, then looked deliberately forward. "I won't let myself be compromised again."

Christine nodded but didn't reply.

No matter how much Tina might say that she was safe, that she was protected and immune from charms, Christine could never trust her completely.

CHAPTER 5

Because it was still early Friday afternoon, coming close to three-thirty, they were able to find parking out on the street. The sky was more overcast now, and the air smelled of iron and snow. Crowds of cars raced along Rainier, all desperate to get home before the weather turned awful.

Tina pulled out her phone and paid for street parking via an app. Christine watched, curious. Even Dennis didn't have one of those. Then again, he'd go six blocks out of his way to find merely zoned parking instead of having to pay for it.

Like Christine, Dennis was frugal.

Christine and Tina decided not to take their lives in their hands by trying to cross the street mid-block, and instead, walked down to the intersection. They passed a fancy vegan restaurant that smelled like rotten tofu, as well as a yuppie brewpub that already had a large happy-hour group sitting and watching some game on the huge TV over the bar.

"Neighborhood is gentrifying hard," Christine commented as they crossed the street. In front of them was a very fancy coffee shop, an upscale consignment store that dealt primarily in vintage clothing, as well as another bar.

Tina nodded. "I remember when I would have had much tougher protection spells at hand walking through this neighborhood," she said. "But now—money's come in. And a lot more will be following it."

"Light rail's just a couple blocks that way," Christine said.

"Really?" Tina asked, wide-eyed. "I wouldn't have thought of that. But you're right. People with good jobs can live here now and have an easy commute to work."

Christine bit her lips together. She would *not* ask if Tina had ever ridden the light rail, let alone a bus. Christine found that she was still angry at the news article that had come out a few months before, reporting about the Seattle city councilmen and women taking a bus together, and how it had been the first time a bunch of them had ever even ridden on a bus.

Yet, *they* were the ones making decisions about public transport for the rest of the city.

"Here it is," Tina said. "The instructions said to tell the people in the bar that we have an appointment." She paused, then pulled out the golden silk bag holding the charms. "Here."

Christine took the coin Tina handed her. It was as large as an old-fashioned silver dollar, with a serrated edge and a small hole in the center. The metal felt cold enough to burn. Squiggly lines ran in concentric circles on the face of it, some language that Christine couldn't identify. The other side held what looked like Egyptian hieroglyphs, also written in concentric circles.

The magic expanded as she held the coin, spreading out in a wide halo. She didn't try to warm the coin any more, and instead, slid the cool metal into her front jeans pocket. She felt the bubble of magic adjust, expanding to fit her from head to toe. Her back (which had fully healed from the attack the night before) felt exposed. The protection wasn't very deep.

If she swallowed the coin, would it protect her more fully? She didn't want to experiment and find out.

Tina gave her a grin. "Ready?" She looked excited, like a schoolgirl about to have a brave adventure, like going to the mall without her mom.

"Ready," Christine said. "And be careful," she said, feeling dowdy in comparison. She was dark and solid compared to Tina's brightness.

But both sides were necessary to make a coin, right?

A desk stood just to the right of the entranceway, but no one was behind it. It looked like an old-fashioned hotel desk. A green lamp illuminated a plastic-coated seating chart taped to the top of the desk. The air swam with the smell of many different types of alcohol; cheap whiskey, hoppy beer, even some rich wine.

The floor was uneven, made of cobblestones, which surprised Christine. Was it smart to have such an uneven floor in a bar? She'd think that was a health hazard. Then she saw the thick rubber mat that had been rolled up and rested beside the desk. That probably smoothed out the floor enough when the bar was open.

To the left, past a short wall, the place opened up. A long bar took up the entire back wall, probably sixteen feet long. The front of the bar was covered in well-polished brass, while the rest of it was made of dark wood. The tables and chairs had all been pushed to one side of the room. A lanky Asian guy mopped the floor on the empty side.

"Bar's closed," he said without even looking up.

Christine marveled at how dedicated he seemed to be to his cleaning. Was it a form of meditation for him? Or was he just trying his darnedest to ignore them? The scent of the pine cleaner fought with the bar smells. It lost the battle.

"We have an appointment to see Lunar Honeycomb," Tina said. She held out the printed receipt.

"Huh," the guy said, still mopping. He turned his back to them, finished the far corner, then stuck his mop in the industrial bucket beside him. He pulled a cloth out of his back pocket, wiped his hands, then finally came over to them.

He smelled spicy, like a good curry. His black hair was all held tightly in a man-bun at the top of his head. He had a tattoo of a pair of koi fish circling his arm, colorful even in the dim light. He peered at the slip of paper then nodded. "This way," he said.

Tina shot Christine a grin, then nodded her head in the direction of the guy, as if to say, "He's cute, right?"

Christine shrugged. Maybe. For a human. Not really her type.

The guy led them out of the bar, then turned left, past the three bathrooms that stood with their doors open, the smell of bleach wafting out from them. He took them through a door marked, "Staff Only" and down a tiny hallway. Christine felt as though she took up most of the space. Bare bulbs hung down from a sagging ceiling. She hunched in on herself, trying not to touch the pasty green walls, afraid she'd get slime on her bright red coat.

They stopped in front of a door with a glittery star square in the center of it. "He's in there," the Asian guy said, then he walked away without another word.

Tina looked at Christine. "Just be prepared," Christine warned her.

Tina gulped and nodded, then got a look of fierce concentration on her face.

It made Christine smile. Tina knew better than to start glowing, but she was just one step shy of it. Christine almost felt sorry for this Lunar Honeycomb person if he tried anything.

Immediately after Tina knocked, a booming male voice said, "Come in!"

Christine still didn't feel completely prepared. She wished she'd watched at least one of this performer's videos.

But it was time, ready or not.

∼

The room held a strange perfume. Was that what theatre makeup smelled like? Overlaying that came the scent of sickly sweet incense, which Christine spied burning on the makeup table.

The room was tiny, and stuffed to overflowing with costumes hanging from racks lining the walls. Dozens of shoes were carefully aligned under the movable metal clothing racks.

The mirror above the makeup table had bulbs framing it. It was the only light in the room. Lipstick, open pots of blush and concealer, as well as at least a dozen brushes and pens lay strewn across the top of it.

But the room was strangely empty. Where was this Lunar Honeycomb? He'd told them to come in, right?

Christine turned slowly. She could see well enough in the dark, but this place had some sticky shadows.

There. Beside the door. She stared hard at the darker shadow she saw.

"Ah, very good!" came that deep, booming voice again. "Clever of you to spot me so quickly," he added as he stepped out from his hiding place among the costumes.

Christine felt her eyebrows raise. Tina had warned her, but that was different from seeing it in person.

He wore a ballerina's costume made of pale pink satin, complete with a tutu. Between the thin straps holding up the top, Christine could see his broad, muscled, hairy chest. He had a huge black mustache that curled up at the ends, like a circus ringmaster. On top of his bald head, he wore a shiny tiara, held in place by a thin band of elastic looped around the back of his skull.

Christine considered for a moment before deciding that he looked good in that particular headgear. He'd chosen one that was taller, which made his face seem thinner and longer.

"Are you Tina?" Lunar Honeycomb asked, looked at Christine. "No, that's you, isn't it?" he added, coming forward to shake Tina's hand enthusiastically. "It's so good to meet you! Thank you for coming to my humble abode." Then he turned and said, "And you are?"

"Christine," she said, suffering to have her hand pumped as well.

"Sisters, right? Though not twins," he added, looking from one to the other.

"Sisters," Christine told him firmly. It was a better, and easier, explanation than the truth.

"And you want to find out about your Destinies?" Lunar Honeycomb said. He walked over to the costumes on the far wall, then reached past them and pulled out a folding table.

"Yes, we do," Tina said. She raised her chin and gave him a stubborn look.

Christine could see Tina preparing herself. While Christine hadn't sensed much power in Lunar Honeycomb, she could still understand what had disturbed Ty.

This guy seemed…slippery. Not like a shadow demon, but perhaps related to them.

Lunar Honeycomb set up the table as well as two folding chairs. He pulled out a bright red silk cloth and flapped it down, covering the table, before he sat on the makeup table bench, facing them.

Tina took the chair on the left, while Christine took the other. She pulled forward slightly, automatically putting herself in front of Tina, as if to protect her.

Lunar Honeycomb raised a single black, bushy eyebrow, but didn't say anything. Instead, he made a circling motion with his right hand.

Suddenly, a mirrored glass ball sat in his palm.

Christine stirred, uncomfortable. Had he made that ball appear using magic? It hadn't felt like that. She sniffed, but she couldn't smell anything beyond the dark scent of glitter and their own lavender charms.

Lunar Honeycomb offered the ball to Tina. She hesitated, then took it, also looking uncomfortable. The darkness pressed in on them, the air in the room growing thick and still.

"Do you have a Destiny?" Lunar Honeycomb asked. The words pressed against Christine's skin, cool like a misty day.

"I did," Tina said.

Christine's heart pounded hard. Tina already sounded drugged.

"Please pass the ball to your sister," Lunar Honeycomb directed.

Was Christine going to have to drag Tina out of here? She looked so dazed. She held out the ball wordlessly to Christine.

Christine stiffened as she took it.

Lunar Honeycomb, himself, had no power.

This ball of his, however, packed quite a magical punch. And somehow, this Lunar Honeycomb was tied to it.

She remembered Ty telling her how sometimes the court would order a criminal's powers to be bound to an object, thereby creating a magical artifact.

Was Lunar Honeycomb a criminal? Were all his powers bound up in the glass ball? If so, why did he still have it?

"I see," Lunar Honeycomb said after a few moments of Christine holding the ball.

Christine wouldn't have been surprised if he called her a troll, if he could see through her own magical disguise when she was holding the silver ball.

"Tell me, *sister*," Lunar Honeycomb said with a strange emphasis on the word.

Yup. He knew she wasn't human.

"Do you have a Destiny?" he asked.

Christine felt the words ringing solidly in her core. Huh. She didn't have to answer. There was no compulsion behind the question.

Still, it was designed to bring out the truth.

"I do," she said solemnly, knowing the words to be true.

"Well, it's obvious to me what happened between the pair of you," Lunar Honeycomb said after he'd retrieved his magical ball and hidden it away again.

Christine didn't trust him to speak the truth without the ball there. However, she would still listen. Then use that mountain of salt, as she'd promised Ty.

"You stole your sister's Destiny," he said, pointing at Christine.

"No, I think the demons did that, when they kidnapped her and tried to twist it to their own purpose," Christine replied hotly.

Lunar Honeycomb shook his head. "No, M'Lady," he said. His tone sounded so mild, even as he disagreed with her.

But it told her that he did, indeed, see her for who she really was. Not just a troll, but troll royalty.

"There were a series of monuments destroyed last summer," Lunar Honeycomb said. "Covered with ugly, demon-spawn graffiti. Speculation was that they held powers that the court had bound. Perhaps your powers," he added.

Christine neither agreed nor disagreed, careful to keep her face neutral.

"I think you two always had a twinned destiny," he said, waving an indulgent hand, indicating the pair of them. "But as you picked up your powers, and you destroyed the places holding them, you also destroyed your sister's ties to her Destiny."

Christine shook her head. No, that didn't make sense. Ming had bound her powers illegally. How could he have bound Tina's Destiny at the same time? The changeling spell hadn't been cast yet. Besides, the human Oracles had declared Tina's Destiny muddled after Lars had kidnapped her. And it had been many months later before Christine had started collecting her powers.

"The Oracles did originally say that my Destiny was tied to great powers," Tina said slowly. "My parents always assumed that meant that I would have great power, that I needed to train diligently and grow as strong as possible."

Christine shifted in her seat, uncomfortable. That would be one way of looking at that prophecy. That Tina's Destiny had been tied to Christine's powers would be another way.

"You see!" Lunar Honeycomb declared gleefully. "You did destroy her Destiny when you claimed your powers."

"No," Christine said, shaking her head. "While I agree that we probably do have twinned Destinies, that doesn't mean that mine cancels out Tina's. Or vice versa."

Tina smiled sadly. "It's okay. I should have known. You're the chosen one. Not me."

"But—" Christine tried to object.

"She's right. I can see it," Lunar Honeycomb said.

Christine opened her mouth, then shut it again. Why did humans have to have such an either/or approach to everything? Why couldn't both Tina and Christine be extraordinary?

But she wasn't about to convince Tina just then.

Hopefully, however, Tina would recall her own unique abilities. Before it was too late.

"Look, just because this Lunar Honeycomb guy said you no longer have a destiny, doesn't mean he's right," Christine said. She held her own temper in place, though she wanted to shake Tina. But that would have been a bad idea, particularly since Tina was driving and the traffic had gotten worse.

"I don't want to talk about it," Tina said curtly.

"But—"

"No," Tina said. She clenched her jaw so tightly Christine was afraid she'd freeze that way.

The rest of the ride back to Christine's apartment was filled with icy silence.

"I'll still see you on Sunday? Lunch at my parents' house? 2 PM?" Christine asked before she got out of the car.

Tina hesitated, but then she nodded slowly. "Do you need a ride?"

Her question loosened the tight feeling in Christine's chest. "No, I don't. But thank you," she added. She'd go by portal, leaving from the one up the block and appearing at the one at the dock close to her parents' house.

Christine walked slowly into her apartment, thinking about what Lunar Honeycomb had said. She couldn't believe him, not one hundred percent.

But she'd always had a niggling feeling that there had to be a reason why, when she'd freed her powers, she'd accidentally destroyed the locations where they'd been kept. She hadn't meant to tear up the fire station, or destroy the delightful fountain. She couldn't repair those, though she was doing her darnedest to repair the fairy bridge. At least she hadn't toppled any of the pillars where her earth power had been kept. The landscape all around the monument had been destroyed, though.

She was so close to finishing the bridge. She looked at her phone after she reached her apartment. It was late enough that she could have a quick dinner, then go down to the park and work for another couple hours.

As Christine left her apartment a strange smell wafted over her. She stopped and sniffed the air.

Damn it. Those shadow demons were still around.

Had they been sent by someone to harass her? Had their first encounter not just been random chance?

She looked around, but she didn't see them. She focused on the small boxwood hedges that grew on either side of the door, but she didn't see any magical disturbance either. They weren't hiding in the shadows.

Still, what was she going to do if they tried to ambush her when she came home? And why were they still after her?

CHAPTER 6

Christine grew tense as she walked down the darkened street to her apartment. She could smell the damned hyenas though she couldn't see them. She'd worked on the bridge until late that night.

She arrived at her apartment unscathed. What the hell were those things playing at?

Nik had left her a message about getting to the shop by 11 AM, so Christine didn't have a chance to go back to the fairy bridge Saturday morning. However, the night before, she'd carefully taken a dozen pictures so she could show Nik her progress. As well as to see if she could prompt him into giving her more tips.

There wasn't a good bus that she could take to the International District. She could get there by the light rail, but that meant a hike up to the Capitol Hill station. She could also hop on the streetcar, but that went such a circuitous route that it seemed to take forever. It was always much easier to get there, and to Nik's shop, using a portal.

However, the damned portal was blocked again. Christine found herself growling under her breath as she stomped away, back down the alley and up toward Madison. Maybe if she was lucky, she could catch a bus to Broadway, then get on the streetcar.

Most of the International District was considered neutral territory. No fighting was allowed between the races there. That was why there were demon bars as well as *kith and kin* havens. She wondered if that was also why Nikolai had originally built the portals to his shop in that area as well, extending the neutral territory.

Because it *was* neutral territory, one side or the other, or even the other (if she considered that there were three sides to this conflict: humans, *kith and kin*, and the Host) was always putting the portals in the area out of commission. They'd remain unpassable for a few weeks until the court got involved and ordered the portals opened again.

Were all three sides all just hoping that the beings who traveled through that portal would give up? Would the beings who used the portals stop reporting that they were down, since they seemed to be always down?

Christine still called the hotline to report it. (And yes, those portals were really down a lot if the court had set up a special hotline dedicated to complaints about them.)

The operator sounded bored and told her that the court already knew that the portals were closed. He assured Christine that they'd be open again soon, but Christine didn't believe him.

It turned out Christine was lucky, and got to the bus stop just as the right bus pulled up. However, as she expected, that meant she'd just missed the streetcar, and it was a good twenty-minute wait before the next one.

With a sigh, Christine considered her options. She could walk down Broadway and straight into the International District. It was a much more direct route than the one the streetcar took. The air was chilly again, though the snow had held off.

It was coming. Soon.

Christine trudged along, passing construction on one side and yuppies on their way to Saturday morning brunch. It wasn't that she hated walking. However, she was built for endurance and strength, not speed. Walking always seemed to take so much time! It wasn't like she was Tina and could just skip along.

Although…

Christine stopped and pondered for a moment, upsetting the bearded gentleman coming up quickly behind her, making him swerve and curse under his breath.

He probably thought she needed to work out more. That her curves were fat, not muscle. Or, heaven forbid, that she wasn't smiling enough.

Christine reached for her earth power as well as her air power. Could she get them to cooperate, at least for a little while? To work with her and make her life just a little easier?

The air power agreed to puff her up, while her earth power would push her along.

Suddenly, Christine found herself moving along quickly.

Too quickly.

And she wasn't walking either.

However, rather than squabbling with her powers or getting them to slow down, she created an illusion: she made it appear as if she floated along on one of those silly looking wheels. She'd seen them before, zipping up and around the hill. They were a single wheel with a long piece of wood sticking out of the center of it. She placed her feet on the wood while the wheel went zooming along, like from that old cartoon about cavemen she'd once seen.

Much to her delight, the illusion worked. Some of the people she passed threw her envious looks, glancing down at her feet.

It thrilled her that she actually got her magic to work with her for once.

Soon, she cruised down the hill, under the freeway with the koi painted on the pillars, past the non-working portal, then across and up and into Chinatown.

A few blocks away she stopped at a building that was still boarded up. It looked like it had at one time been a school or a church. White marble steps led up to a boarded-up door. The large, once white sign proclaiming, "Notice Of Proposed Land Use Action" was well covered by graffiti. The previous tags had been plastered over and now a series of ducks done in gold paint walked across the sign. Garbage piled up around the entrance. At least Nik didn't let the homeless sleep on the steps, so the place didn't reek of urine.

Christine easily called up a portal to the Emporium. It sprang up quickly, a large blue oval tinged with white lights. She knew that any of the humans walking by wouldn't see anything: When she'd come here with Dennis, he hadn't even realized there wasn't a proper door.

Stepping through the portal gave Christine a sense of relief. Her powers liked it here. While the International District was supposedly neutral, it felt as though fights were erupting behind closed doors, setting her on edge. Wild magic streamed through the air, chasing the smells of fish and garlic.

How close was the Great War? More clashes between demons and *kith and kin* were occurring. Rumors of huge armies gathering on the shadow worlds were rampant. Was it just a matter of time before they attacked the human plane?

Christine felt guilty about her part in furthering the Great War. She'd blocked the main road to the worlds of the *kith and kin* by destroying the fairy bridge, which meant that kingdoms and sovereignties were allowing more portals and risking attack. However, the demons had taken out two of the other roads after the bridge had been destroyed, so it wasn't all her fault.

Christine wasn't sure how she could learn more about the plans of the demons, or if she even wanted to. She had told herself that she had more important things to do, like rebuilding the fairy bridge. But now she wondered if her ignorance was going to cost her much more.

Nik's shop looked much the same as it always had. The ceilings were especially tall, so giants didn't have to shrink after they entered. Bright white crystals covered the ceiling. They had a special spell enchanting them, so they would shine with the desired light of the shopper.

It had surprised Christine to learn that she liked bright lights when she shopped. It was the only time, however. The rest of the time she much preferred dim lights.

Posters advertising various products covered the tall walls. Nik would change them out now and again. She realized that he'd done it recently. There were many more protection spells, charms, and amulets being advertised now. She snorted when she looked up at the one that had an "elf" on it who looked suspiciously like that now-famous, white-haired fellow from the movies. He was, of course, selling healing spells.

Tall shelves organized the store into aisles. The only change that Christine had managed to get Nik to make was to add a small set of bookshelves over in the corner. The books on magic as well as guides to the various races sold slowly, but there was enough turnover that Nik agreed to keep the shelves stocked.

Spell ingredients filled most of the rest of the space: gold coins for holding temporary charms; innocuous-looking travel mugs with hidden compartments; bins of agates that rustled when she walked by, ready to break apart anything magical.

Nik stood behind the counter up front, talking with a tall, only partially visible creature. Its black cape kept fading in and out of this plane. As Christine drew closer she realized that the being had a white mask on, hiding its face.

It wasn't here to rob the place, was it? But Nik talked casually with it, asking about the creature's hometown.

Christine nodded at Nik, then let herself behind the

counter and through the dark purple curtains that separated the shop from the backroom.

She paused and took a deep breath once she let the curtain fall. The backroom smelled comforting, of old books and dirt, and of sticky sweet lemony magic that Nik used to clean the place sometimes. It also had a faint scent of fresh pine, which Christine always assumed was the smell of Nik's sweat. If a wooden man could sweat…

Shelves rose from floor to ceiling and filled the walls in the backroom as well. Mostly, the shelves contained the items that Nik ran out of quickly and was constantly having to restock, such as tiny, velvet amulet bags, cages for carrying crickets and other small (live) insects as well as the plastic boxes that could be used to kill creatures humanely before using them in spells.

Several cardboard boxes lay piled up in the far left corner. Christine walked over and looked at one but didn't touch. All fifteen of the boxes were labeled (1 of 15, etc.) and came from the same estate, Mr. Ilcvash's.

She grinned. Maybe this was why Nik had been so eager for her to come back to work. He'd bought yet another estate and needed the inventory organized.

She shook her head. While Nik had been a shopkeeper forever, he still didn't have the knack for filing that she did. No one in her family did. Not Tina, either. Christine wasn't sure where her ability and desire for order had come from. It didn't seem very "trollish" to her.

What Nik did have was the ability to look at something and know its value to the right customer. If you needed anything, anything at all, Nik was the one who could find it for you and sell it to you at a price you could somehow afford.

Nik finally came into the backroom just as Christine was looking at the boxes again, trying to decide if she could maybe, perhaps, open just the corner on one. She knew better, though. There was too good a chance that Nik had spelled the boxes and that something nasty would happen if she tried to open one without him there.

"Good, I'm glad you've waited," Nik said, nodding toward the boxes in the corner. "Come. I want to show you something."

He waved his hand, as if swiping a window clean. The boxes suddenly felt less mundane. Instead of being plain cardboard moving boxes, they looked fancier, with hand-drawn scrollwork along the edges. They were still cardboard, she thought, but reinforced with something else. And they all still had their labels and numbers on them.

Nik pointed to box number three, which Christine easily lifted from the stack. Nik gave a low whistle. "You've really built up a lot of strength working on the bridge, haven't you?"

Christine thought she might have, but she didn't have a lot to compare it to. It wasn't as though she'd grown up in a troll body.

"I'm close to being finished," she told him as she put the box down at his feet. "Want to see?"

"Yes, please!" Nik said. He sounded excited. "Being able to go home would release a lot of the tensions that some of the *kith and kin* are feeling right now."

Christine swallowed down her guilt as she pulled out

her phone. "Any suggestions?" she asked after Nik had swiped through the pictures a couple of times.

Though Nik kept his face neutral, she could still tell that he wanted to say something. "What is it? You can tell me."

He nodded and after a moment paged back to one of the first pictures. Christine had focused the camera on where the rocks connected to the earthworks on the southern side. Then he expanded the picture and zoomed in on a spot close to the middle of the rocks.

"Here," he said, pointing. "The rest of the bridge looks solid. But that feels like a weak point to me. I could be wrong, it could be nothing. I hesitate to say anything when I'm not one hundred percent certain."

That he said anything meant that he was pretty certain, however.

Christine nodded and swallowed her disappointment. She'd been hoping that Nik would tell her that she'd done a marvelous job. Of course, he would find mistakes that she needed to fix.

"Other than that, it looks wonderful," Nik did add. "You've really found your stride, haven't you?"

"I have," Christine said, smiling as she took her phone back from him. It had been so satisfying these last few days to make good progress. The rocks weren't fighting her at all now, and slid eagerly into place.

"You'll be finished in the next day or so," Nik predicted. "Then what?"

Christine swallowed. She was afraid to say anything out loud, as if that would set her plans in stone.

Or jinx them.

"I need to travel to Trollville," she said after a few moments, while Nik waited patiently. "Then, after that, I don't know."

And that was the biggest part of the problem, wasn't it? As a human, when she'd been under the changeling spell, she'd never thought much about the future. She'd been forced into limbo, and stayed there for years.

Now, though she didn't want to be in limbo anymore, she really wasn't sure where she was going next either.

"I see," Nik said softly. "You know you always have a home here, right?"

Christine smiled at him. Technically, he wasn't family. He wasn't *kith or kin* or of the Host or anything else.

He was something much better: Found family.

Christine looked curiously at the ledger book that Nik had handed her from the third box. It had a black binding that smelled of leather, but didn't. She wasn't sure what sort of material the binding had been made of, why it had that slimy feel to it.

The first page, the first column listed names. Mostly human names, but a few others as well, possibly orcs, definitely brownies, as well as some she didn't recognize.

None of the columns were labeled. After quite a few of the humans' names were dollar amounts. Were they paying bribes? Paying off debts?

Nik pointed to one of the names: Al'ber du Pain, with a sign like an eye next to it. "I recognize that as a demon name. Pretty down on his luck. Panhandles next to the light rail station sometimes."

Christine traced the line with his name across the page. Sometimes the column held a big zero. Many times it held a single mark, counting off something.

"I kept thinking and looking at that, wondering what in the world Al'ber could give someone. Anyone. Not money." Nik paused and looked at Christine again.

She swallowed hard suddenly. "He's a demon. Was he stealing souls?" She found her voice had come out in a hoarse whisper.

Nik's face remained remarkably emotionless. "Yes, that was what I feared." He reached for the ledger.

Christine gladly closed it and handed it to him. A horrible thought struck her: Was the leather binding not made out of cow leather, but of something else? Some*one* else?

"Nik?" Christine asked softly as Nik held the book closed against his chest and stood completely motionless, like a statue. It kind of freaked her out. For a wooden man, he always seemed so animated.

"Nik?" Christine tried again. "Are there other people you know in there?"

Nik seemed to deflate at the suggestion. "There are," he said. His voice sounded strangled. "Court officials."

Christine groaned. The shit was really going to hit the fan now. "What are you going to do?"

"I don't know," he said. "I assume that this wasn't a trap, that it wasn't created for us to find. I think it's authentic."

Christine nodded. Nik had a point. Demons were

notoriously devious. Of course they would create false trails for people to find.

"Was this estate that of a demon? Did all the boxes come from there?" she asked.

"They did," Nik said. "However, it's been sitting in one of my warehouses, protected, for at least three years."

Christine had often wondered about the size of Nik's warehouses. Given his general lack of organizational abilities, it didn't surprise her that he kept finding more boxes that he wanted her to go through.

"I should turn this in to the court, or at least, to a special prosecutor," Nik said slowly. "Someone who isn't appointed by the court, or elected, so they have a level of impartiality."

"And then what?" Christine asked, concerned. It wasn't like Nik to sound so dead.

"Let the chips fall where they may," Nik said. She didn't like the grim tone Nik's voice held. "Though I'm afraid it will bring on the Great War sooner rather than later, if some of these officials are removed."

He turned and looked at her over the ledger book clutched to his chest. "You need to finish that bridge. This weekend. Before Monday."

"I will," Christine said. "I—"

"No," Nik said, interrupting her. "I won't have you foresworn. Don't make a promise that you might not be able to keep. Particularly if it turns out that the fault I found is a serious one."

Christine nodded, pressing her lips together. She had to finish the bridge. Get on with the rest of her life.

Though it did feel as though she was a baby bird being

pushed out of the nest and told to fly, despite the fact that she'd never used her wings yet.

Christine studied the area of the fairy bridge that Nik had pointed out to her. What was wrong with it? What had he seen?

She'd gone from the shop directly to the park. Though she wore three layers—long-sleeved shirt, sweatshirt, and baggy hoodie—she still felt cold. That wasn't usual. Then again, it didn't usually snow in Seattle. The clouds above her threatened to dissolve into a myriad of flakes soon. It was already snowing in the passes. The highway going through the mountains was closed.

She reached out to touch the bridge, then ran her hand over the stones. They felt colder than before. Was that just the weather? She raised her head and sniffed. She smelled the local traffic, and the new grass that had foolishly poked above the ground when the sun had come out. About half a mile away, park rangers had been building new trails, and she could smell the fresh pine chips they used.

But she didn't catch a whiff of those stupid demons. No, they were going to ambush her outside her apartment. She growled.

The bridge trembled in response.

Christine pulled her hand back, startled. The bridge needed to stand on its own. She couldn't have any part of herself, even a trace of her powers, still trapped inside the stones.

Had that been what Nik had seen?

Christine walked out from under the bridge, then up the earthen side to the top. She knelt down on the forgiving earth and reached out her hands, touching the stones.

Ah. There. Just a foot out from the start of the bridge, and to her right. There appeared to be a soft spot.

She'd put that together before Nik had showed up. What had she done wrong, there?

Her wind element brushed against her, skating out across her outstretched hand. It swirled a pattern in the dirt above the spot, marking it for her.

Puzzled, Christine reached out and put her palm solidly on the spot. Then she pushed out with her senses. Huh. The spot felt *wet* to her, not like solid rock. What had she done there?

She thought back, trying to remember. There had been an issue with mud, and she'd used more of her water power to dampen the dirt, then tried her fire power to dry it out.

Seemed she'd left too much water and magical residue there.

What could she do?

Her air power circled around again. Why was it being so helpful? Christine didn't trust that element. She still owed that element a "future favor." Not knowing what the favor would actually be made her queasy.

But Christine wasn't going to turn away the help being offered. She pulled from the earth, her strongest power, then pushed out with the air, blasting the section at her feet dry.

It didn't take long to dry it out. To test it, Christine went back under the bridge, put her hand up on one of the spans, then growled again.

The bridge remained firm, standing separate from her.

She'd have to remember that, to not put so much of herself in her work. Not unless she wanted to be tied to it forever.

CHAPTER 7

Christine chose to not place the last two stones that would have completed the bridge. While on the one hand, it would have been nice to finish, on the other hand, she wanted to share the accomplishment with her family and friends.

Instead, Christine carefully set the two rocks down on the top of the span of the bridge. It was almost time for Sunday dinner at Mum's house. She adjusted her appearance, cleaning off her jeans some, before she strode purposefully away from the bridge and toward the Japanese Gardens, just across the street.

The snow still held off. She didn't know if the weather was waiting for something, some big event. It felt that way. Then she shook her head, telling herself that she was just being paranoid.

The trip via portals to her parents' house went smoothly, dropping her off on the pier about half a block from her parent's house. She quickly walked to the end of the bobbing platform and stepped onto solid land. She'd never liked the water that much. Turned out she was a mountain and earth person instead.

Mum came out of the kitchen when Christine entered the house. "Hello, darling!" Mum said. She held up her hands, showing that they were both full at the moment. "Come and make yourself useful!"

"Sure thing!" Christine made her way into the kitchen. It smelled heavenly, of rich mashed potatoes and spicy meat-and-carrot stew.

The kitchen had a small eating nook on one end, with a modern, open floor plan on the other. For a while, they'd had an island in the middle of the room, but that hadn't worked at all and had made Mum cross every time she had to walk around it to get anything.

The stove was on the right-hand side, with the lovely fridge beside it. The sink was in the center at the far end and the countertop spread wide on either side of it. All the cupboards were painted a bright white, and the countertops were made from a marble with a mosaic pattern that had large splashes of red. Cheery yellow paint covered the wall.

"What can I help with?" Christine asked, looking around expectantly. She had assumed that Mum would have everything under control. She usually did.

"Beat these, please?" Mum asked, pointing to a bowl containing half a dozen eggs. The hand eggbeater lay on the countertop beside the bowl.

"Okay," Christine said. It felt good to be useful. That was something she'd discovered when she'd been making progress with the bridge. Or even when she'd spend time organizing Nik's stuff. It had been one of the reasons why being an archivist had appealed to her so much: the organization system was strict, and she rarely had to deal with people.

"Electric mixer's broken," Mum admitted as Christine started whipping the eggs with the beater.

That made Christine grin even wider. Mum was getting used to having a daughter who was so strong.

"Now, I know you think it makes us uncomfortable to see your true face," Mum said softly as she chopped the celery for the salad. "But how are we going to get used to it if we never see it?"

Christine sighed. She'd been trapped, unable to leave because of the task her mother had given her. Mum was very clever that way.

On the one hand, Christine doubted that her mother would ever fully accept her troll daughter. But Mum might be right, as well. If she never saw Christine's other face, she would never have a chance to get used to it.

"You know, Mum," Christine said, pausing for a moment. "I could start with just a few pieces of my troll face. Maybe the tusks and the ears. Let you grow used to those first, and only gradually keep the transformation going"

Mum thought about that for a moment while Christine went back to beating the eggs. "How stiff do you want them?" she asked.

"Foamy," Mum replied. After another short pause, Mum said, "All right. Show me your partial face."

Christine nodded and put aside the beater. She had to think about this in order to get it right. She exposed her tusks, both the longer ones that reached up from her lower jaw and the smaller ones that hung down. She broadened her face and darkened her skin. Then she let her ears show, tall and pointed on either side of her face. She still considered them one of her better features, even if they couldn't move or swivel on their own.

Mum took a deep breath, then abandoned her cutting board to walk over to Christine. She peered up at her daughter, looking more curious than repulsed.

"You can touch me," Christine assured her mom.

Mum nodded and hesitantly reached up, brushing her fingertip along Christine's eyebrow, then up to the tip of one ear. She looked down at Christine's bare arms. The skin there had also changed, showing more of her troll's tough hide.

Then Mum stepped back. "Now, I'd like to see all of it," she said. She sounded very determined.

Christine shrugged. With a flick of her hand, the entire illusion disappeared. She braced herself.

At least Mum didn't gasp. Instead, she paused for a brief moment before she said, "Fascinating. I can still see you, your human face, you know. Both faces share some of the same features." She thought for a moment before she added, "Honestly, I like you better this way. Pure. Not mixed."

Christine deliberately smiled at her Mum, showing off her ragged teeth. "Are you sure?"

"Of course I am," Mum said dismissively. "And I think you're very attractive in whatever form you take."

Christine didn't roll her eyes at that, even though it sounded as if Mum had practiced the phrase so it came out smoothly.

They talked quietly, working side by side, bonding in that quiet way mother and daughters do. By the time the doorbell rang, Christine had forgotten that she wasn't wearing her illusionary face anymore.

"That's either Ty or Tina," Christine said, wiping her hands off. "I'll go get the door."

Ty stood poised just outside. He stiffened when he saw her, then sniffed deliberately. "Are you okay?" he asked. He wore his puffy blue-down jacket and brown leather conductors' cap. Instead of jeans, he appeared to be wearing nice brown slacks, with loafers.

"Oh. Oh! Yeah. My mum wanted to see my true face," Christine said, finally realizing what Ty was asking about.

Ty beamed at her. "Smart woman, your mum," he said. He held up the bottle of wine he'd been holding. "I'm sure she'd appreciate this, too."

"Awesome. Thank you," Christine said. "Please, give me your coat. Just be warned that if you join us in the kitchen, Mum will put you to work."

Ty grinned and told her, "I'm looking forward to that."

Christine left Ty in the kitchen with Mum when the doorbell rang again, then had to go through the same routine with Tina, reassuring her that everything was fine even though Christine was in troll face. At least Tina appeared to be fine, and was still friendly. However, she had a sad air about her.

Christine would bet that Tina was mourning the loss

of her Destiny, feeling lost since she was no longer the only special one. Christine just wanted to shake her and tell her to get over it, get over herself. Tina was still amazing even if she didn't have a singular Destiny.

Although Christine still doubted what Lunar Honeycomb had told them. She was certain that Tina would still play a very important role in the Great War coming up.

Or she would, if she could start believing in herself again.

Soon after Tina arrived, Dad came in with Dennis. Dennis wasn't up to driving yet, so Dad had gone to fetch him.

"We're in here!" Mum called out as, of course, everyone stood around in the kitchen, snacking on the veggie tray she'd been preparing, drinking the excellent red wine that Ty had brought. Christine had even had a few mouthfuls before putting it to the side. It was good, but it still wasn't her thing.

Dad came in and beamed at everyone, shaking hands with Ty and giving both Tina and Christine a big hug. "You sure are looking swell!" he exclaimed after he let Christine go.

Really, who else but her dad used the term "swell"?

Dennis had stayed by the doorway. His arm was in a sling and he still looked too pale. The navy blue shirt he wore just seemed to wash him out.

"Fourteen stitches, I heard," Ty said, walking over to Dennis, ready to shake his hand.

"You should have seen what the other guy looks like," Dennis said, the joke sounding weak.

"Doc says you'll live, though, right?" Ty asked, still holding onto Dennis' hand.

"Still around to bother you for a long time? You bet," Dennis replied. He pulled himself up straighter. "Smells heavenly, Mum," he said over Ty's shoulder.

Ty shrugged and backed away, coming to stand next to Christine. He gave a brief shake of his head.

Christine almost felt relief. At least her brother wasn't infected with shadows or poisoned by demons or something. But she couldn't let herself relax. Not yet. She could tell that something in the house still bothered Ty

It wasn't until they'd started carrying food out to the table that Ty finally made the connection. He whispered in Christine's ear as he passed her going into the kitchen.

"Something's wrong with your dad."

Christine made elaborate plans all through dinner about how to get her dad to Nikolai's Magical Emporium. However, she suspected that all she had to do was ask, that he'd be happy to go meet her friend Nik, whom he'd heard so much about.

She nearly didn't make her own announcement, but in the end, decided she had to. It was too important for her to miss.

"I have something to say," Christine said, rising from the table when everyone was finished eating.

"Don't tell me. You're gay, too, on top of all this," Dennis joked.

Christine rolled her eyes at him. If she'd been seated

close enough, she would have thwacked him. Particularly the way his comment made Tina stiffen up.

"No, you idiot." Christine paused and took a deep breath. "I'm almost finished with the bridge."

"That's wonderful!"

"Swell!"

"Good job, sis!"

Christine beamed at all of them. "If you'd like, you can come with me to the park and be there when I place the final two stones."

"It would be an honor," Ty said.

Christine couldn't help the joy she felt. She was still worried about her dad, but he seemed the same as he'd always been. Had one of the Sorgenfrey demons influenced him again? Or was it something else?

They all bundled back up in their warmest coats and headed out. Both Tina and her dad drove to the park. Christine rode with her parents while Ty and Dennis rode with Tina. She felt kind of like a kid again sitting in the backseat behind her father in the old family Subaru.

"How are you feeling, Dad?" Christine asked as they started up the hill.

"Me?" he said, sounding surprised. "I'm doing super well. Never better. A bit worried about your brother, mind you," he added. "But I think he'll pull through. And extremely proud of you, young lady." He caught her eye in the rearview mirror and winked.

"Thanks, Dad," Christine said. She'd put back on the illusion of her human self when they'd left the house. She was glad that her dark skin probably couldn't show her blush.

"Yup. I knew that building that bridge might present a challenge, but that you were up to the task. You can do anything you set your mind to, you know? You're just one of those people."

Christine sat back in her seat, slightly puzzled. Did her dad really believe that she could do anything? But there had been so many things she hadn't been able to do as a child, had never wanted to take part in. Social things. Large family gatherings.

And yet…

"Thank you," Christine said. She reached up and squeezed his shoulder. He patted her hand and they drove through the quiet streets, everyone who could do so hiding from the coming storm.

They parked in the parking lot next to the Japanese Garden, then made their way across the street. Christine remembered the first time she'd come to the bridge, that dark night, with Ty. How she'd felt out of balance, overfull with just two of her elements, and yet still lacking, still *hungry* for the others.

Her powers had lost some of their individual voices over the past months. However, they didn't work together well. Also, it was difficult for her to figure out how to use them. She needed another troll for a mentor.

This afternoon, the bridge looked more solid than it had that first time. A dark, rough arch across a now empty river. The abutments on either side were down to just rocks and dirt. Hopefully this summer, the grass would grow back.

All of the ground underneath the bridge was muddy and full of gravel. Christine had tried to use as many of the smaller pieces as she could to make the connecting mortar between the stones. But she'd dug up a lot of the dirt in the process, drawing the stones up from beneath the earth. Again, by summer, she hoped that grass and wildflowers would hide the remaining scars.

No one stood near the bridge. She'd strengthened all her protection spells this last week, making sure that no humans would stumble onto the bridge before it was completely finished.

Everyone looked at her expectantly, though Mum snapped a few photos on her phone.

"Go that way," Christine said, pointing the group at the left side of the bridge. While they trooped up that side, she walked up the other. The two stones she needed to finish the bridge lay closer to her side than theirs.

"It's beautiful, darling," Mum said, taking more pictures.

Christine beamed at them. She was proud of the work she'd done. It wasn't completely finished, she still needed to add a short stone wall to either side, a type of balustrade, so that idiot human children wouldn't fall off.

But those weren't as important as the span being finished.

She picked up the two rocks that remained, one in either hand. With trepidation, she walked out onto the bridge. It held, and it stood on its own, separate from her. Then she bent over and carefully placed the rocks in the two remaining holes, like finishing a jigsaw puzzle.

The bridge thrummed under her feet, as if a thunderous train suddenly passed underneath. Bright blue light sprang up, singing softly between the rocks, filling in any remaining gaps.

Just as quickly, the light died and the bridge grew steady again.

Christine glanced to her right. The world looked hazy in that direction. She knew that if she drew closer to it, the regular world would disappear and she'd see the world of *kith and kin*, the start of the road to Trollville.

Then she blinked. Wait. There was *another* world there, a different tollhouse. It looked to be in the middle of a flat field, with purple spiky flowers growing along the path. The scent of sharp curry wafted in from it.

Then she remembered. The fairy bridge, while it was primarily a conduit to Trollville, could also connect to other planes.

She drew a huge sigh of relief. The bridge was working!

"I give you, the fairy bridge!" Christine announced as she returned her focus to the people standing at the far end.

Mum started politely clapping, with the rest joining in. Then Ty couldn't stand it any longer and he strode out onto the bridge, coming to Christine's side.

"This is wonderful," he said softly. "Thank you for fixing this. I wouldn't have led you here if I'd known exactly what this bridge represented."

Christine nodded. They'd talked about it before, how Ty almost always traveled using portals. He'd never used the fairy bridge before. And the magical element of the bridge had been effectively cloaked.

"It's okay," Christine told him. "And it's fixed now." Though the project had taken her much, *much* longer than she'd wanted it to, she was still mostly finished. One more day to build the balustrades.

And then...

CHAPTER 8

C hristine gave her mum and dad one last hug, sending her human family home. She planned on working on the bridge a bit more, starting to add the side walls. Tina excused herself as well. Which was too bad, as Christine had hoped she'd have the opportunity to talk with Tina about her Destiny.

Tina had seemed subdued all evening. Was she bummed because she no longer had a Destiny? Christine would never say something like, "Welcome to the rest of us." Tina had depended on her Destiny to make her feel special, instead of feeling exceptional just on her own.

Was that what Dad had meant? That Christine was capable, just in herself, whether she was human or troll?

And when had she become so confident in herself?

Ty stood below the bridge and handed up large rocks to Christine. They didn't talk much, though sometimes Christine had to say, "No, not that one, the one by your foot" when it came to the proper stones. Ty had an okay feel for what rocks went where. Was that the magic contained in the rocks? But he didn't have Christine's touch.

Cold winds blew at them, promising icy sleet. Christine tasted the storm in the air. The world had already grown dark, night closing in.

Christine built the first third of one of the walls before she was ready to call it a night. She knew that Ty would stubbornly go as long as she did, up to and past the point of exhaustion. However, she'd finished the main part of the bridge. Connected the worlds.

The rest was just—prettification.

Christine stood up and stretched, groaning as her back muscles complained about being overused. She was going to have a really long, hot soak tonight. "I think that's it for tonight, Ty," she called down.

He didn't respond.

"Ty? Ty?" Christine asked. She leaned over to look at Ty.

His face had partly changed, his long snout pushed out and covered in tan fur, with a black nose and sharp, pointed teeth. Tall ears (that could move on their own!) stuck up on either side of his conductor cap. His eyes had fully changed, golden with an elongated pupil.

He stood with his nose up, sniffing mightily. He moved out from under the bridge and stood a few feet away, hunting the scent.

"What is it? What do you smell?" Christine asked. She jumped to her feet and raised her own nose, trying to figure out what it was.

Crap. It was those shadow demons. Their smell blended well with the scent of the coming storm.

Or were the two connected, somehow?

A demon materialized out of nowhere beside Christine. It was only partially there, however, as Christine learned when she slashed at it and her claws only found air.

Ty howled, loud and angry, below. What were the demons doing?

Christine ignored the two, no, three demons who wanted to engage with her at the edge of the bridge. Instead, she leaped over the short wall she'd built, landing solidly on the ground. It cushioned her automatically.

All her powers rose up, angry. They hated these stupid shadow demons as much as she did.

Why were they here now? Was it because she'd finished the bridge? There didn't have to be a general announcement about it, she knew. The magical thrumming the bridge made connecting the worlds was probably felt on most of the planes.

Christine growled as loudly as she could when she saw that at least half a dozen of the shadow demons surrounded Ty. "Cowards," she taunted as she raced forward. "You need to pick on someone your own size."

The shadow demons were idiots for attacking her here. All the rocks near the bridge bore her name. Many of the larger ones had been part of the original bridge, and still had the royal sigil burned into them.

Christine threw a slurry of rocks, gravel, and mud at the first two attackers. Though they were only partially on the physical plane, she had enough magic in her volley to get through to them. They howled in pain as the rocks struck them. The ice from her air element drove spikes through the shadows.

There wasn't any way for her to reach through and just grab one of the assholes. That wasn't how her magic worked. Still, she froze the next demon with a bunch of frozen spiderwebs. She figured it would hold the demon longer if there was more than one.

She tried blasting the next with cold air, but that just made the idiot turn and grin at her. It lunged and Christine found herself backing up, dodging claws that would suddenly appear and disappear.

Finally, she levitated a rock and used it to block the next claw attack. The stone disintegrated into dust at the impact.

Damn. She hadn't realized the creatures were so strong.

However, before the demon could vanish again, she reached out and grabbed the wrist of the hand in front of her. Then she yanked, hard.

Seemed that if she had a strong enough grip, she could pull a demon out of the shadows and onto this plane. Though it wasn't just her physical prowess—her earth element also helped her to ground the asshole in the here and now.

Two punches to its ugly snout and it was out, cold, and not going to bother anyone else.

Ty had managed to down one of his own opponents, but his jacket was torn to shreds, the fluffy feathers floating around him like snow.

No. That *was* snow.

Christine used her air element to push away the snow from Ty, to give him back his sight.

Now the shadow demons had not just the night to hide in, but the storm as well.

"We've got to get out of here!" Christine told Ty. She threw more rocks and ice at the demon immediately in front of Ty, driving it away. "Come on!"

She reached for his arm.

Too late.

An icy cold wave slammed down on Christine, engulfing her, as though a bucket of frozen water had just been upended over her, like one of those videos she'd seen where celebrities got doused for charity. She suspected that *this* ice water was much colder, enhanced magically to instantly freeze her.

She tried to reach for Ty but her arm had frozen.

Ty, too, couldn't move.

Christine pushed her senses deep under the earth. The ground wasn't frozen. She could still draw power up. Though her air power was sluggish, her water element merged with the falling snow and added to her strength. Christine raised a series of rocks, all with the royal sigil burned into them, around Ty and herself. She didn't know how effective the barrier would be, but it was better than nothing.

But that was about all she could do. She didn't have the power to break her body free.

She struggled against the spell, ignoring the laughter she heard, belittling her efforts.

It was that stupid Lars Sorgenfrey. He came walking

into view, from her left. "Struggle, my dear! It's so cute to see you being ineffective," he said as he strode forward.

Christine sighed and stopped her effort for a moment so she could more effectively glare at him. "What do you want?"

"World domination. Hell on earth. To twist the souls of all Cubs' fans by having them lose yet another World Series. The usual," he said.

He looked like a movie star with his perfect blond air, chiseled features, and piercing blue eyes. He wore a thick black wool coat that came to his knees. She bet he was wearing only a T-shirt underneath with some stupid saying on it. His jeans were new, pressed, with the crease still showing, and his black boots reflected what little light there was.

At least he stayed in his human form. The courts had seen to that, forbidding any in his family from transforming into their demon selves while they stayed on this plane.

It wasn't much of a punishment. Christine had wanted to see them all back in prison, but they'd found a more sympathetic judge who'd gone easier on them than the first one had. Which she thought was just a crime, given how they'd kidnapped Tina and then tried to twist her Destiny.

On the one hand, Christine was glad that she lived in a non-capital punishment state, at least as far as the court for *kith and kin* was concerned. However, she occasionally wondered about the wisdom of that now, particularly when it involved demons like the Sorgenfreys.

"Why are you here?" Christine demanded when it

appeared that Lars wasn't about to answer her first question.

"In general, because I'm going to make sure that the demons win the Great War, and become the rulers of not just you puny people, but all the planes as well," Lars said with his typical, stupid, frat-boy grin.

Christine just rolled her eyes at him. Of course, he wasn't about to answer one of her questions.

"Why are we standing at this piss-poor attempt at building a bridge? You'll see," Lars said.

Christine growled. She kept trying to find a way to break the damned spell holding her. Could she just push her sense of self down deep enough into the earth and escape that direction?

"There he is!" Lars said, walking past Christine.

Damn it! She couldn't turn around. She couldn't even turn her head to see Ty, though she suspected he was fairing far worse than she. While she didn't like the cold, her tough troll hide protected her from it. She suspected his fur wasn't anywhere near as effective.

She hadn't been struck by any of those damned poisonous demon claws. Plus, the spell held him more tightly than her, or else she knew he'd be cursing up a continual storm by now.

A familiar presence came into her range of vision.

Joe. Her old boyfriend. The only other troll she knew in Seattle.

He stared at her as he came up. Why was he so angry? What had she done? Or rather, what lies had Lars told him? Falsehoods that he must now believe, based on the hate in his eyes?

"I'm sorry, Christine," he told her, though he didn't sound sorry at all.

Then he resolutely walked past her. He studied the bridge for a moment, before he scampered up top.

He appeared to be staring at that one spot that she'd had to fix earlier, that Nik had pointed out. Was it still weak?

Joe knelt down on the rocks. She knew they'd accept him and wouldn't bite into his skin, though she wished they would.

Without another word, Joe *pounded* down on the rocks with both fists, directly in the center of that soft spot.

Christine groaned with the bridge. There was still something soft there, something she had needed to fix.

Joe hit the area with first one fist, then the other.

Christine panicked. He was going to destroy all her hard work! It was going to take her forever to rebuild the stupid bridge. Then he'd probably just come back and destroy it again.

She struggled to free herself. Could she move her hands? Her fingers? Hell, could she even twitch her nose?

There. She breathed in deeply. Her water power, which always felt to her like one of her weaker elements, gave her more oxygen. She found her chest moving, the cold backing away from the fire that burning in her belly.

Just a few more deep breaths, and she'd start to break free.

No. Don't. Don't stop him.

What the hell?

Christine paused and looked deep inside herself.

It was her air element. It had been frozen as well. It bore the look of a wall of ice.

Let him finish. Let him destroy the bridge. You owe me a future favor.

"What?" Christine demanded. "You're kidding me. Why now? Why this?"

Let us help you rebuild. All of us.

"What the hell do you mean?" She wasn't sure if she was speaking out loud, though Lars hadn't turned to look at her.

Joe had punched a hole through the top of the bridge and now gleefully tore the rocks apart. Abortive sparks of magic flickered as the rocks disconnected from each other.

Christine couldn't contain her groan. She must stop him before he got too far!

Wait. See.

The image her air power showed her was a marvel. With her air and water powers working together, the rocks floated up from the ground. Christine's earth and fire powers welded them back together, making them stronger than they had ever been.

Christine herself stood on the ground next to the bridge, conducting the movements, the flow of rocks and magic.

"*Why didn't you tell me this before?*" Christine demanded. She was stunned at all that her elements could do to help her with the bridge. All they could have done.

You didn't ask.

That brought Christine up abruptly. She *had* asked.

Okay, so maybe technically, she'd demanded.

However, Christine saw the flaw in the air elemental's

plan. "I'll be trapped there," she said. "The bridge—there's no way to remove all of my magic from it. I'll be forever tied to it."

Exactly, her air element purred.

Why was that a good thing? Yet, Christine felt the appeal. It meant that she would forever be traipsing between the other planes and this one. She would literally have a foot in all worlds.

Was this the future favor her air element had always had in mind? That Christine spend her time traveling between the planes?

Her air element had promised that the favor she requested would be something that Christine would want to do as well.

And though she wanted to be freed from this bridge, she'd also grown to love it as well.

"I will not stop him," Christine promised her air element. She would allow Joe to tear apart her bridge.

She continued with her deep breaths, building the fire within her, willing it to melt all the ice holding her. Once she'd freed herself, she reached out and took Ty's hand.

He stared at her with wide, wild eyes. She'd be willing to bet that he hated being held so still more than most.

She pushed her fire at him, warming first his hand, then causing the heat to spread through all his limbs.

With a final shudder, Ty broke free. He shook himself all over, like a dog shedding water. Then he glanced over at the now re-broken bridge. Joe had torn a gap between the two ends of the bridge and was widening it steadily.

Ty looked back at Christine, puzzlement clear on his half-dog face.

Christine just nodded back, hoping she looked more certain than she felt.

By the time Lars had turned back to them, Christine had her defenses ready. She threw a circle of rocks to surround Lars, hemming him in.

"Won't work a second time," he told her smugly. Then he tried to move. He jerked from one side to the other, but he couldn't break himself free. "Damn it!" His face broke out in a sweat. "You shouldn't be able to do this," he muttered.

"Oh, I could break you in two, little man," Christine lied. She knew she couldn't, but she wanted to see him sweat. "But I'm going to let you live. For now."

She knew that technically he'd thrown the first punch by binding her. Still, it didn't feel right to strike a bound opponent.

"Come on, Ty," Christine said, turning away.

Joe continued his destruction of the bridge, oblivious to the drama being played out behind him.

"You can't just leave!" Lars complained.

"Sure I can. No one said I had to stay through the final, pathetic act," Christine threw over her shoulder as she and Ty started to walk away.

"I'll destroy the bridge again if you rebuild it!" Lars yelled after them.

That made Christine stop and turn around. "And I'll rebuild it every time," she told him quietly. She took a quick breath. Glanced at Ty. He still looked puzzled.

Christine felt deep in her bones that this next step was the right one. She knew the gravity of what she was about to say, the commitment she was about to make.

She said the words anyway, despite the consequences.

"I promise."

The words echoed deeply in the earth, recorded there for all time. The reverberations forced Lars to shift his feet.

Christine didn't laugh at how uneasy he looked, though the satisfaction she felt kept her warm for the rest of the night.

CHAPTER 9

Christine's alarm went off *way* too early the next morning. She blindly groped for the clock, remembering at the last moment to *not* merely pound on the offending thing.

She'd already broken two clocks that way since the changeling spell had ended. She really didn't want to buy yet another a new one.

She pushed herself up to sitting, rubbing at her eyes. It seemed too dark for it to be time to be awake. She glanced at the windows over her bed.

Gasping, she rolled out of bed and raced into the living room, where she had the best view.

Snow covered all the glass, making the world seem gray. Christine shivered. The snow wouldn't last for long, however, it would certainly make a mess of everything.

She called in to her work, relieved when she received the standard recording that the library was closed due to inclement weather.

That meant she could go back to the park. Maybe rebuild the bridge in half a day or so.

A pounding on her door stopped her from making plans.

More chills ran up and down her spine.

Now what?

Christine marched into her bedroom to grab her robe. "I'm coming, I'm coming," she told the impatient knocker. "Sheez."

As she feared, a messenger stood there. Older than the first one she'd met, maybe in his early fifties, with a grizzled face and wisps of gray hair standing up all around his head. He wore a gray bike messenger jacket with yellow stripes down the side. Though he had a pair of snowshoes strapped to his backpack, he also had a silver and blue bicycle helmet dangling from one arm.

How had he made his way here? Did he bike where he could, and then snowshoe the rest of the way?

"Christine Tuckerman?" the man asked.

"Yes, that's me," Christine confirmed, though she'd been tempted to lie and to tell him that her roommate hadn't made it home the night before.

But she wasn't sure how that would go over with the court.

The man handed her a heavy, white linen envelope with something written on the front.

Wait. Both her names?

Before she could ask, the man intoned in a booming voice that echoed weirdly in the enclosed hallway: "Christine Tuckerman, also known as Princess Kizalynn Linumok Te'Dur, you have been served with papers requiring you to appear before the court of the Host on this day of the LORD, at 11 AM."

"Really, do you need to go through all the theatrics?" Christine asked, glancing around nervously. She had new neighbors across the hall. She didn't want to get on their bad side by having weird visitors at all hours.

Though maybe they would just have to get used to it. She had lived here long before they had moved in.

However, the older man replied in a gruff voice, "You have been served, m'Lady. I'm just the messenger."

Christine couldn't help but smile at someone using her title that way. "Thank you," she said.

He looked a little surprised. She would bet that not many people thanked him for delivering his messages.

"You might want to leave early for the courthouse," he told her as he started strapping his helmet back on. "It's kind of nasty out there."

"Won't a portal just appear in my living room or something?" Christine asked, surprised. She'd been hoping that she wouldn't have to go anywhere.

The man grimaced. "Can't break the sanctity of the home," he told her. "Plus, this place is too well protected."

"Ah, I see," Christine said, though she didn't. She merely had the one charm in the living room, as well as a *ba gua* mirror hanging directly in front of the door, so no one who meant her harm could enter that way.

Didn't mean that demons couldn't just transport themselves into her place willy-nilly. Did it? Or had her charm grown stronger with age, as she'd continued to live here and do magic?

She was going to have to remember to test that theory, sometime. Maybe Ty would help.

After the messenger left, Christine went into her living room. At least this time, she'd be prepared for a visit from an angel.

Well, maybe merely better prepared. As prepared as she could be.

She seated herself in her most comfy chair so she wouldn't land on her butt again when the angel appeared.

The back of the envelope was closed by a heavy seal formed out of red wax. The symbol looked like a pair of wings with a sword underneath.

"Here goes nothing," Christine said into the chill morning air.

She held the envelope out at arm's length, then broke the seal. Bright white light streamed from the envelope.

The light coalesced into an angel, complete with wings and halo and shiny sword.

Then it began to speak.

⁓

Christine took an extra-long hot shower. Not because the angel had been slimy or anything like that. But she suspected that the court always sent the messenger most likely to *disturb* the one receiving the message.

And angels, pure angels, were disturbing as hell. Particularly for those who were *kith and kin*.

So Christine took her time, standing under the pounding hot water, trying to reclaim a sense of calm and rightness.

She didn't know what she was being summoned for. Was it because she'd left Lars imprisoned by a circle of rocks? Surely he'd broken free by now. Though she snorted at the image of him cursing up a storm as the damned shadow demons tried and failed to break the rocks apart.

Besides, she doubted he'd do something as stupid as that. Not when Ty had the scars to prove that he'd been attacked by the shadow demons. Not when she could point to the broken bridge. And she had witnesses who could testify that she had finished the bridge, and then someone else had torn it apart. (Mum had taken a myriad of pictures.)

No, it had to be something else.

Suddenly, Christine felt cold, despite the hot water still pounding down on her.

Had Nik turned in the book? Was she being called to testify about that?

It was the only thing she could think of.

Damn it! At least she hadn't actually promised Nik that the bridge would be fixed by today. Though it had been, before Joe had torn it apart.

Poor Joe. Though she was pissed off at him, she also felt sorry for him. Lars had twisted something in Joe's soul for him to turn against his people that way.

Or had Joe always been corrupted?

That gave Christine another pause.

She tried to remember exactly what Joe smelled like. Because while he carried the scent of good fertile dirt, he also smelled like *other*. Something that was distinctly not troll. That second faint scent had always made her keep her distance from him.

Was that the demon influence she smelled? She didn't know.

But she didn't blame him for turning against her.

No, that was all on Lars' pointy head.

Christine finished her shower and dressed as nicely as she could, given the numerous layers she was putting on.

The cold outside bit into what little exposed skin she was showing. Why was it so cold? Or was this weather demon-enhanced, which was why it stung her so badly?

Winds had piled up the snow into any crevice they could find. Christine encouraged her own air element to push back and to weaken the drifts so Christine could get through.

It still took her almost fifteen minutes to walk four blocks. She was sweating under her many layers.

And she still had far too many blocks to go.

Christine reached the King County Courthouse five minutes before 11 AM. She'd been lucky that at least some of the main sidewalks had been shoveled, particularly near the hospital as well as the shops there.

Still, she'd had to walk carefully. A solid inch of ice lay hidden by the snow.

"We're closed," a dour guard told Christine as soon as she pushed her way into the hallway of the courthouse.

"But I have a summons!" she automatically complained. "Delivered this morning! For 11 AM!"

The guard shrugged. "No one in the court right now," he said. He gave her a sneer for good measure. "You should have figured that everyone would have problems getting here."

Christine opened her mouth then shut it again.

This was a human guard, who worked for the human court. He had no idea that the courthouse held a portal to the court of the Host.

"Can I just stand here a minute and warm up?" she asked, trying to sound plaintive and not demanding.

The guard deliberately looked at his watch. "You have one minute."

Christine pressed her lips together to prevent herself from growling at him. He was merely human. Nothing demony about him. Just an asshole.

She took one more step into the hallway and planted herself there, clapping her hands together and stomping her boots, trying to bring feeling into her feet.

She'd been in cold before. There was just something unnatural about the current weather.

Perhaps the guard wasn't always so scummy, either. Maybe he was also being influenced.

She glanced over at him. He had his hands on his waist, his fingers twitching, as if he wanted to bring out his nightstick and just hit her.

Naw. He was just a bully and liked ordering people around.

When her one minute was up, the guard told her, "You need to go now."

Christine sighed and made a show of buttoning up her jacket, putting on her gloves, and adjusting her scarf, taking up another whole minute.

"Now, miss," the guard said, trying to sound menacing.

Humans were so cute when they tried to be mean. They had no idea, though, how to properly growl at someone.

She wasn't about to show him, though.

Instead, she pushed her way slowly through the revolving door.

Magic scented the air—a faint whiff of persimmon and cinnamon. Along with the scent of paperwork and bureaucracy.

On impulse, Christine pushed her way into the hallway again. "I was just wondering—"

"Go!" the guard directed.

Christine pushed at the revolving door again, watching the light turn golden. Instead of stopping when she reached the street, she went around and around, three times, the light growing brighter and brighter.

Suddenly, the light faded and Christine was elsewhere.

Guards stood on either side of the doorway to the courtroom. They didn't look happy. In fact, they looked as pissed off as the human guard above. The one to the left had a ram's head instead of a human face, with yellowed horns curling on either side of his head. The other looked more like a wild boar, complete with nose ring and hooves for hands.

They wore plain navy blue uniforms with many implements hooked to their large utility belts. Christine recognized some of the items they carried, like the stun wand, the silver chains of binding, as well as the regular old pepper spray. Nik sold them in his shop.

Others, however…was that really an orange squirt gun? Did it carry holy water for uppity demons? She wondered at the wooden stakes as well.

The rest of the hallway looked like every government office hallway she'd ever been in, with scuffed beige walls, cheap gray linoleum that was yellowing along the edges, and plain wooden doors.

"Court has yet to start," said the one with the ram's head. He had a surprisingly high voice given the broad expanse of his chest. "You are expected, M'Lady."

Christine nearly did a double-take at that. How had he recognized her? It wasn't as if she was wearing a tiara or something.

Then again, she was one of the very few trolls in Seattle. And the court had summoned her using both her names.

"Thank you," she said, aiming for gracious but probably failing and hitting school-girlish instead.

Christine walked into a courtroom that looked almost identical to the other two she'd been in. Opposite the entrance, a dormer stuck out from the far wall. Underneath that was another set of closed doors.

In front of the doors the bench (and counter) where the judge sat. No one was there yet. Two steps down, on either side, was a long table. To the right sat three demons who looked as nasty as any of Christine's nightmares. To the left sat three angels, who were just as disturbing as the demons with their bright light and always smiling features.

As she had feared, Nik sat up front at the defendant's table, talking earnestly to a woman Christine recognized. But from where?

Finally, she realized it must be Hannah Cameron, the lawyer whom Nik had originally sent her to. She still had that long, horse-like face, though she'd let her dishwater blonde hair grow out, flowing down to her shoulder blades now. She wore a power suit of course, this time in an incredible pale blue color.

Christine wasn't sure how anyone could make that suit look so awesome. Unless, of course, Hannah was using some sort of spell?

It had never occurred to Christine that Hannah couldn't be human, no matter what appearance she presented. Hannah recruited non-humans for the Great War. None of the *kith and kin* would trust her if she was actually human.

Christine smiled, pleased with herself when she finally recognized the glimmer of magic circling around Hannah. Though Christine had no way of knowing what race Hannah was—her disguise was too good.

Maybe Christine would have to ask Nik sometime.

Nik glanced up and nodded at her, but didn't wave her over. That disappointed Christine. However, it also made sense. She found a seat in a half-empty row near the back. Three pixies sat there, their human forms buzzing with excess energy. They still wore daisy crowns, vests, and gauzy petal skirts, like rejects from the Renaissance festival. All their features were exaggerated, with sharp noses, long chins, and overly pointed ears. Christine knew that in their true form, they had nasty fangs and sticklike fingers tipped with poisonous claws.

However, pixies were generally friendly, and would come to the aid of a human who treated them well, particularly the humans who followed the old ways and left the pixies crumbs of cake and thimbles of milk. The pixies looked a lot rougher than they were.

Christine sat primly on her seat. The court was usually quite punctual. Where was the judge? Why hadn't the court been called to order?

More people came into the courtroom, filling the seats. Demons, angels, *kith and kin*, even a few humans. Were all these people here to testify for Nik? Or against him? She tried to get a reading on the emotion in the room, but that had never been her strong point. She was a troll, not an empath.

Finally, the bailiff came out from a door next to the judge's bench. He looked as though he was related to the ram's head guard outside, though his chest was three times as big and his meaty hands looked as though they could deliver a hefty punch.

"All rise!" he called, banging a large staff against the wooden floor of the platform.

The demons and angels sitting on either side of the judge's bench rose with everyone in the courtroom.

"The Honorable Judge Newman," the bailiff proclaimed. He had a great voice, the kind that belonged on a late-night radio announcer for a jazz station.

Christine tore her attention away from the bailiff to the judge. He had that look about him of a man up to no good. His face was weaselly, with dark pocked skin and slitted eyes. He wasn't fully human, though he presented as such. She wondered if all judges were part demon, part angel, so that they would be able to equally represent both sides.

Would Hannah ask for a change of venue, if this judge was compromised? Could she?

Or perhaps he was one of the few judges who weren't in Nik's book, which was why he scowled at the entire courtroom.

"Let the preliminary arguments begin," Judge Newman said.

Christine wished they would just announce what the court case was about. She had to put it together from the various arguments, however.

It seemed that Nik had brought the demon ledger to the court, requesting special immunity, particularly from everyone listed inside the book. A judge had granted that, but it would hold only as long as those whose names were in the book testified that they'd owed this demon something.

The first up was a brownie. Christine had never gotten along well with them. They had such an attitude problem, particularly when it came to trolls. Every brownie she'd met at the store had been nasty and belligerent to her. They all tended to wear the same outfit, and this brownie was no different, with short breeches that ended just below his knees, wooden clogs that had been dyed brown with pretty painted pink-and-white tulips decorating the top, and a short jacket.

His face was as pocked as every other brownie

Christine had met, with a huge nose that had at least three warts hanging off it. He had bushy eyebrows and flabby lips, and spoke with a lisp.

"Yes, yes, I was in yer book," he said as Hannah flipped open the page to show him where his name had been recorded. "But Ise paid my debt, I has."

"Let the court record that there are, indeed, just two pages where Mr. Hatherhorty had his name recorded," Hannah said. "But what did you pay Mr. Ilcvash for?"

The brownie sighed and looked up at the judge. "Me um was sick!" he proclaimed. "We needed the money!"

"So Mr. Ilcvash loaned you some money, and this book records you paying back his loan?" Hannah inquired.

"Yesh, yesh," the brownie nodded. "'Tweren't nothing more than that. Good loan shark for a demon. Honest. Mostly."

"Thank you," Hannah said. "You may step down."

The three pixies went next, all three of them with a similar story.

It was only when Hannah called up one of the demons that the tale changed.

"I recruited for him," said the bull-headed beast. His torso was flayed and blood dripped down his chest. However, it never reached the ground. Was the blood actually an illusion? Or did he just have a really good cleaning spell that ran all the time?

"So these numbers here, these represent souls?" Hannah asked.

"Of course," the demon said, obviously proud of his work. "At least one a month. Sometimes two."

"Human souls?" Hannah inquired.

The demon tipped his head first to one side, then the other. "Eh. Mostly. Sometimes others. *Kith and kin.* Though Mr. Ilcvash didn't pay as well for those." He made a face.

Christine couldn't help her shudder. She knew that demons were evil, and angels were supposed to be good. But they all were trying so hard to beat each other out that the lines between good and evil blurred. Were there other ledgers out there with lists of angels recruiting as well, in exchange for credits or gold? It wouldn't surprise her.

After forty-five minutes of testimony, the judge declared a break. Christine risked the press of people going up to talk with Nik, finally pushing her way through.

"You okay?" she asked when she saw him.

He wore a plain white shirt, something she'd never seen him in before. He always wore flannel. The fancier shirt didn't suit him at all. In addition, he obviously had toned down his "emoting" spell, so his face seemed, well, wooden.

"I am fine, Christine," he said.

Damn. He even spoke in a wooden monotone.

"How's work on the bridge?" he asked. Did he suddenly sound more hopeful?

"I finished it," Christine told him. Before Nik could congratulate her, she added, "And then Lars and Joe tore it back down."

Was it just her imagination or had Nik's eyes just grown larger?

"Oh, no," he said in a hushed voice. "That's awful."

Christine nodded. She alternately felt angry and heartbroken. "But I'll build it again."

"And they'll destroy it again," Nik said.

"And I'll rebuild it. I promised," Christine said.

Nik just shook his head. "You shouldn't have."

Christine shrugged. "Why was I summoned here?" she asked. "My name's not in the book, is it?"

Nik gave her a ghost of a smile. "No, I was just covering all my bases. In case someone challenged the veracity of the book, wanting to know who else had seen it."

Other people edged in, wanting to talk with Nik. "You need anything, anything at all, you let me know," Christine told him earnestly before she turned and went back to her seat.

The people who had already testified streamed out of the courtroom. The room had just a few benches still filled when the bailiff called everyone to rise again.

Christine waited through the entire afternoon, only to be called close to the end of the day. The bailiff used both her names, which kind of thrilled her, particularly in that deep, sexy voice of his.

Were there male trolls with the same sort of voice? She hoped she'd find out. Soon.

Hannah did a double-take when she saw Christine, as if she hadn't realized who exactly Nik had requested.

Or maybe it was just the whole "princess" thing.

"You are an employee of Nikolai's Magical Emporium?" Hannah asked, consulting her notes.

"I am," Christine said. They'd finally formalized their arrangement at the start of the year. Since it was a barter exchange, neither of them had to pay taxes. However, such deals were recognized by the Host and others as legitimate partnerships, and so needed to be recorded as such.

"And what do you do, exactly, Princess Kizalynn?" Hannah said.

Christine wasn't sure why Hannah would prefer using Christine' royal title to her human one, but this was a court of the Host. Calling her Princess made the inquiry feel more formal.

"I provide filing and organizational services," Christine said. "Nikolai helps me with my magic."

An audible sigh went through the room. Christine realized that she was an oddity—only troll royalty had magic, and there weren't that many of them.

"I see," Hannah said. "Wouldn't it be better to learn magic from a troll?"

"It would be," Christine said. "And I hope to soon."

"You completed work on the fairy bridge between here and Trollville last night, didn't you? Then you destroyed it. Why?" Hannah asked, her voice suddenly harsh.

"I did *not* destroy the bridge after I finished it. Lars Sorgenfrey trapped me and Ty Brooks in a spell. Then another troll destroyed the bridge," Christine explained, trying to hold back her ready anger. How dare anyone accuse her of destroying all her hard work?

"What other troll?" Hannah said.

Christine sighed. She didn't want to incriminate Joe. But she couldn't protect him. He was going to have to face the consequences of his deeds. "Joe D'Angelo," Christine said.

A murmur went through the court. Christine knew that a warrant would be issued for his arrest shortly. And he'd probably be thrown in jail, too. The court would have done that to her, after she'd destroyed the bridge, if she hadn't also promised to rebuild it.

She couldn't help him. He'd made his choice, siding with Lars instead of her.

"And what time did this *other* troll supposedly destroy the bridge?" Hannah asked.

Christine hadn't checked her phone for the time until after she and Ty had left and were headed back to their respective homes. "About six-thirty last night."

"What would you say if I told you that Lars has an alibi for that time?" Hannah shot back.

Christine blinked, surprised. Why would Hannah already know that? Why would anyone have looked into that already?

"I promised him that I would rebuild the bridge every time he tore it down," Christine responded hotly. "That should also be recorded."

Hannah shook her head. "You what?"

"I promised that I would rebuild the bridge," Christine said. "The oath was recorded in the earth. Troll royalty keep their promises."

Hannah turned toward the judge. "Your honor?"

He nodded. "Let me check."

Christine didn't trust this judge one bit. She was going to ask for someone else to verify if he came back and discounted her word.

However, Judge Newman unfroze after just a few moments, his expression as dour as ever. "She did make that promise. At 6:24 PM."

"When were you planning on starting your work?" Hannah asked.

Christine shrugged. "I would have started this morning, but I was summoned here." She couldn't keep her frustration out of her voice. This day had seemed like nothing but a waste of time. Nik hadn't made up the entries in that book. It was real. The things people were accused of were real.

And she had real work to do.

"Thank you for your time, Princess Kizalynn," Judge Newman said. "You are dismissed," he added before Hannah could ask any more questions.

"We have proved the veracity of the book in question to my satisfaction," Judge Newman announced as Christine found her seat again. "The court will now take into custody those accused of misdeeds by association in the ledger."

The demon advisors as well as the angels appeared to be upset by that. Judge Newman held up his hand before they could protest. "There may well be extenuating circumstances in some instances. And I am willing to hear those cases. But we need to get moving. Bailiff!"

The ram's-head man turned toward the judge.

"Issue warrants for those named in the book who haven't testified," the judge declared. He caught Christine's eye. "I believe that those who are guilty won't be allowed to cross the rebuilt fairy bridge."

Christine gulped. How was she supposed to be able to judge that? Could she build in a guilt detector when she rebuilt the bridge?

"All rise!" the bailiff declared. "Court is dismissed until 9 o'clock tomorrow morning."

Christine sagged where she was sitting. She obviously had more work to do that night.

Hopefully, however, rebuilding the bridge wouldn't be so painful this time. Or go so slowly.

CHAPTER 10

Snow blinded Christine when she stepped through the portal at the Arboretum. What was wrong with this place? While it was cold but not really snowing outside of the park, it felt like the park itself was in the middle of a snow globe being shaken by a giant.

Christine pushed on, leaving the Japanese Gardens (the gate was closed but her air power lifted her right over) and heading across the street to the fairy bridge.

It broke her heart to see the stones half-buried in snow. She sniffed the air, looking for shadow demons, but the wind kept shifting. She wasn't sure that she'd smell them even if they were near.

The broken ends of the bridge stood out starkly against the white. At least the stupid demons hadn't tried defiling it or something. Or so she hoped.

Christine trudged through (knee-deep? Seriously?) snow, up to the right embankment. She tugged off her warm glove and placed her hand on the cold dirt.

As she'd feared, a spell lay buried underground. It

LEAH R CUTTER

didn't feel very strong, and had the taint of ice. It was meant to make the earth sluggish so it wouldn't respond to her commands.

Did they really expect that to slow her down? Amateurs.

Her earth power blasted away the spell, cleaning the earth in the wink of an eye.

Then Christine slid her hand up to touch the stones of the bridge. The demons hadn't been able to remove the royal sigil burned deeply into each rock, though she could tell they'd tried. A few of the rocks bore scars, testimony to their mistreatment.

Tenderly, Christine cradled one such victim. The outer layer of the magic it bore had been tainted by the demons, though the core running through it was still pure.

Unsurprisingly, Christine's earth power rose all the way up, angry at such treatment of a rock. In an instant, the magic of the stone contained flowed clean again, bright blue light dancing from the sigil at its heart.

Laughing, Christine threw the stone up in the air, watching her air element lazily glide it back down into place, touching the remains of the bridge.

Christine reached out and physically touched the tainted rocks, making sure that she got each and every one of them, even the ones hiding in the snow.

She couldn't imagine what would happen if she rebuilt the bridge with stones that were so misaligned and tainted.

Only when she was quite certain that none of the rocks remained infected did she step back to the middle of the long-gone river that the bridge had once arched over.

From here, she could see both edges of the bridge, as well as all the rocks.

Then she took another step back, inside herself.

At the start, it had been necessary to convince her elements that they wanted to work with her, to be with her. They'd squabbled constantly, like bickering teenagers. She'd had to argue with them to get them lined up, more than once.

But now wasn't the time for her to assert herself. Now, she needed to let her powers do the work, instead of trying to do all on her own with occasional demands for their help.

Slowly, the first rocks rose into the air. It always surprised her that that heavy lifting was done in part by her water element. She would have believed it was strictly an air power, but maybe it was because water had a lot of air in it.

Her earth element then directed the stones to their appropriate places. It slotted them in, rotating and turning them as appropriate.

Then her fire coated the rocks, baking them together. She helped direct the flow of magic from one stone to the next, making sure that the bridge stood solid and strong, magically.

She pushed in as much of her sense of "right" as she could while she rebuilt the bridge. Tuckermans kept their promises. So did trolls, and particularly troll royalty. She wasn't certain she could keep those who the court had declared guilty from passing over the bridge. However, an oath breaker would find the bridge difficult to cross, possibly impassable.

The blue flames coating the bridge grew brighter, dancing in squiggly lines from one end to the other. The wind tasted of sweet peppermint and lavender, of wild heather and familiar pine.

Her air power also helped keep the snow at bay. Christine realized that the cold had gotten much worse while she'd worked. If she listened carefully, she could hear the howling of winter demons as they were denied their prey.

Within the hour, the bridge was rebuilt, stronger than ever. Even including the balustrades.

And it was all hers.

Christine let her air power maintain its vigilance and keep the snow away while she climbed up the embankment and stepped onto the bridge again.

It felt different, this time.

Why did the bridge feel older, now, than it had the first time she'd rebuilt it? Maybe that was because so much of her earth power lay buried between the rocks, and that magic was as old as the earth itself.

Blue light arched up over her, forming a tunnel for her to go through. It sang of dancing aurora lights and curtains of stars. Christine found herself trailing her fingers along the tops of both balustrades just so she could hear the celestial music better, feel the bass beat in time with her heart, the trilling notes sending cascades of chills down her spine and raising the hairs along the back of her neck.

About midway across, the fork to Trollville sprang up. It wasn't snowing there, no, it looked like how Seattle was supposed to look in February, with warmer weather on its way, leaves budding and the first spring flowers already in bloom. Just around the bend stood the stone tollhouse, strong and solid.

Could she go that way? What would happen if she did? Could she rebuild the bridge from the other plane, if she had to?

Without planning to, Christine found herself taking a step. Then another step. Then a third.

The stones rose up to meet her, singing her praises. They knew her, knew that she was the true heir of the kingdom.

She should call Mum. Or text Dennis. Or at the very least, Ty, before she just disappeared.

But the path beckoned so seductively to her.

She had to go.

The pathway leading away from the bridge was carved into the hillside of a steep mountain. Huge rocks rose up on her right side, while a steep fall waited for her on the left. Even though it was the same time here as it was in the human world—a little after dark in February—she could see everything very well.

The rock of the mountain was tinged yellow. She instinctively understood that it wouldn't break so much as shatter if she applied too much pressure. If she slammed her fist into it, it would disintegrate into dust. It didn't easily break into gravel or small pieces.

Up ahead, a tiny tollhouse had been built on the path. There was no getting around it: even she wasn't sure she could climb the steep cliff either up or down to avoid the house.

The house was built out of the yellow rock, with a red-tiled roof. It looked like a lean-to, with the three walls poking out of the solid rock.

As Christine approached, smoke suddenly started coming out of the chimney. An old man—no, a troll!—came out of the door, hurrying up the trail toward her. He wore a clean white tunic that still hung crookedly around his neck, as if he'd just gotten up. His breeches were made of a brown linen that came down to just below his knees. Dark coarse hair covered just the top of his head.

His face showed much wear. The right bottom tusk had been broken off with jagged edges. One of his top tusks was also broken. A scar ran along his right cheek, the green skin broken by the gray line.

He stopped abruptly when he saw her. "The bridge? It's rebuilt?" he asked.

"For the time being," Christine assured the man. "There's a demon—Lars Sorgenfrey—who's vowed to destroy the bridge every time I rebuild it."

The man boggled at her. "You? You rebuilt the bridge?"

Christine nodded solemnly. "And I've promised to rebuild it every time he destroys it."

"Promised, hmm?" the man asked. He stroked his

beardless chin. It made Christine smile, as well as wonder if trolls could grow beards. "And might I ask your name?"

Christine paused, considering. She poked at her internal powers, but they couldn't guide her in this. She nodded, then said, "Princess Kizalynn Linumok Te'Dur. At your service."

The man's eyes grew round. Then rounder still. She would have giggled at him if it hadn't looked painful.

"Oh my goodness! My goodness! There were rumors, yes, that you hadn't died. That you'd been magically whirled away. That you'd come back, yes, return!" The man gestured wildly as he rambled. "Oh! Dear! Where are my manners?"

He pulled himself ramrod straight, like a soldier on parade. Then he addressed her with a long string of words.

Christine made herself smile, waiting until he finished before she said, "I must apologize for my lack of ability in my own native tongue. I was…a changeling, until recently."

The man gasped. "Horrible it is! Horrible I say! How the humans keep stealing our young!"

Christine felt her smile grow real. She *knew* that trolls wouldn't just willy-nilly hand over their children!

"So now, I must return to Trollville," she said. "Can you point me in the right direction?"

"Oh, my lady! Of course! Of course! Please, follow me. Right this way. Are you sure you don't want to rest for the evening? Continue your journey in the morning?" the old man said as he started rushing back along the mountain path toward the tiny house. "My name is Rodericket. It is an honor, an honor I say!"

"Thank you, but I don't have much time," Christine said. "I'll need to return before the demon comes and tears apart the bridge again." It was Monday night. He probably wouldn't get around to it until Tuesday night, at the earliest.

How many would be able to escape in the meantime? Return to their homes and reunite with loved ones? Many, she hoped.

"That's terrible. Terrible!" Rodericket said. "Please, do come through the travel room. Normally, I would ask to see your papers or something, but you have none, right?"

"I do not," Christine said. She doubted that the human identification card that she carried would be of any use here, along with the cash.

The room they stepped into was much bigger than she'd expected. Was it magic? No! The house had been dug into the cliff. Though it appeared the wall just stopped, it didn't. On the one side, the house was only a few feet wide. While on the other, it continued for at least a dozen more. The walls weren't smoothed over in the human fashion, but looked rough, showing off the stone.

Tables were scattered across the floor. They looked disused, and probably hadn't been visited since she'd first destroyed the bridge. Red-and-white checked tablecloths covered the tables, made from real cloth, not plastic. Empty vases sat on the tabletops. The chairs were all carved from white wood, and looked strong enough to support even a huge troll.

Opposite her stood a brightly-painted red door. A large brass bell hung over the lintel, obviously there to alert those inside when someone entered.

"Will there be more customers, my lady? Soon?" Rodericket asked.

"I don't know," Christine said, unwilling to lie to the man. "There's still the Great War to consider. The demons destroyed two other bridges, in addition to ours. They're attacking kingdoms when they can. They want to force us to fight." Christine found herself speaking more heatedly. "I will not let them come here."

"You have rebuilt the bridge," Rodericket pointed out.

"I also built the bridge to stop oath breakers," she replied. She still didn't know if that would be enough to stop a demon, however.

Rodericket nodded. "That might do. That might do indeed. Thank you my lady! Thank you! I look forward to seeing you on your return. You will return, right?"

"I must," Christine said. She hadn't told anyone she was coming here, and Ty might not get a friendly reception if he just showed up, hunting her.

"Let me show you the way, then," Rodericket said. He rushed across the room and opened the red door, the bell tinkling merrily.

Christine walked next to him and looked out over his shoulder. The path remained carved out of the side of the mountain, but she saw how switchbacks were built into it, leading down the hill. Sharp pines rose up along the curves. In the very far distance, on the horizon, Christine thought she saw something. More buildings? Was that Trollville? Where her bio-dad was imprisoned? And maybe where her uncle, the old king, ruled?

"Just follow this along," Rodericket said, indicating the single path down. "When you get to the fork toward the bottom, stay to the right side, not the left. There will be a waterfall that you'll have to go under. But in just a few hours, you should be there!"

"Thank you," Christine said.

Rodericket stood to the side as Christine stepped past him, onto the honest stones. They felt so good under her feet! Though she'd never been here before, she somehow recognized it as home.

She took a deep breath of the clean, cool air, smelling the mountain sage and pines. Her earth element thrummed, pulling power out of the ground beneath her, buoying her up.

She hadn't stayed up all night in quite a while. Luckily, she knew her elements would support her in this.

They, too, wanted to go home.

"Thank you," Christine said again as she bowed her head to Rodericket. Then she turned and started down the path.

"Goodbye! Goodbye! See you again soon!" Rodericket called after her.

Christine merely nodded her thanks and continued down her path.

It was going to be a very long night, but finally, she'd get to see her native lands.

The fork in the path was hard to miss. It came at the bottom of the large mountain. If Christine remembered correctly from the previous vista, she was in the foothills now.

The sun would be up soon. The sky was already much lighter. Color had seeped into the world, and Christine could distinguish between green and black. Grass grew at her feet, and she'd spied some of the early, pink flowers. Birdsong lightened her heart.

She knew that there wouldn't be books with lists of birds in them, and pictures, so she could identify them. Most of the *kith and kin* didn't believe in writing things down.

But now, as a princess, maybe she could get them to change their minds…

She was surprised that Rodericket had told her to take the fork to her right. The other looked as though it led directly to Trollville and would be a faster path.

Should she believe him? She hadn't gotten the sense from him that he'd been lying at all. He'd seemed nervous, but more overwhelmed than anything else.

She stood at the fork, then took two steps along the left, just to see. She invited her earth sense to work with her. Could it identify anything?

Her air element started whispering to her. *Clifffsss hidden ahead. Ssssharp dropoff. Unssssseen sssssspacccce. Trapsssss.*

Huh. She hadn't realized that trolls could be so sneaky.

Christine thanked her air element profusely for helping her as she started down the right side of the fork.

Sure enough, it led around the last sharp hill, then went straight across the joined valley. The path widened to a road, maybe a car and a half wide. Christine marveled at the way the stones had been flattened and joined together. Much better than pavement. Though a layer of dust covered the road, making it seem as though it might be dirt or gravel, it was actually really well made.

Christine realized that farms now lined the road on either side. Those fields were cultivated, not wild. She saw the houses off in the distance, away from the road. They looked solidly built, out of stone, of course, not out of wood. They all only had a single story and many of them sprawled, as if new rooms were just added on as needed, instead of being planned.

She longed to explore, yet she also knew she didn't have a lot of time. She'd need to leave again before nightfall. And she had yet to get to the city! It loomed on the horizon, still far too distant.

That gave her a thought. Now that she was on a flatter road, maybe she could conjure up her riding wheel again?

Her elements seemed…amused. Her air and water element picked her up quickly, her earth element propelled her along. The imagined wheel appeared between her feet again, whisking her down the road.

A farmer who was already up and working came into view. He looked up, puzzled at what he saw. Christine merely waved at him and kept going. When she looked back, he'd already gone back to work.

Her heart swelled. Such hard-working people! She was going to love getting to know the trolls here.

～

Christine slowed down when she saw the first horse-drawn cart. It carried a load of seasoned timber, the pine scent tickling her nose. But there was more than enough room to pass him. She waved at the driver. He stared at her, surprised. Then waved back.

More carts and now pedestrians came onto the road after the sun was well on its way. Christine's phone no longer worked, but she'd guess it to be around 10 AM by now. Given the speed she traveled at, she might make it to the city by eleven.

It still surprised Christine to see so many familiar faces. Not familiar in the sense that she knew them, but familiar as in similar to the face she saw every morning in the bathroom mirror. It relieved a tension that she hadn't realized she'd been carrying.

She didn't have a chance to really study the trolls she passed. She had the sense that most of the people on the road were farmers or workers. They wore plain clothes, clean but patched. No one carried swords or wore bows, however more than one did walk with a stout stick which she supposed could be used in an emergency.

She also had the sense that no one had magic. One or two had sparked as she'd passed, but their magic had seemed low-grade and tied to the earth.

Nik (and the others) had been right: very few trolls had magic.

Christine stopped riding along merrily when she got close enough to the city walls to see the guards standing on the rampart. It didn't surprise her that the city was walled like an ancient medieval town. Or that the walls were made of dirt, not stone.

While Christine was comfortable working with both stone and dirt, her earth element preferred dirt.

An enemy would have an impossible time blasting

151

through dirt walls protected by trolls, even if the trolls had very little magic.

No guards stood at the open gates. Christine still paused, touching the heavy wood on either side of the opening, reinforced with iron bars.

It thrilled her when the gates appeared to recognize her. She felt the sigil buried deep inside the wood. Someone from the royal family could magically lock these gates from afar to keep out all invaders.

She stepped away before the sigil rose to the surface and blue light spilled everywhere. She wasn't sure exactly how she was going to announce herself to the king, but she had the feeling this wasn't the way to do it.

She stepped past the gates and into the city.

She was here. Finally. In Trollville.

Farmers and workers streamed in and out of the open gate, both men and women. The road was now paved with smaller stones, all perfectly aligned. She supposed it would be easier to replace the smaller stones rather than the bigger ones when they wore out.

Shops lined the earth embankment spreading out on either side of the gate. The street in front of her was perhaps only as wide as a big car. That surprised her, as trolls were larger than humans. The houses were taller than she'd expected too, almost all two or three stories. They were built out of good stone, though now she was starting to see dark red brick as well.

She passed by a shop serving chicken soup (based on the sign that showed a chicken and a bowl of soup) that smelled heavenly. But she had no money. Maybe when she came back…

Most shops had their front shutters open. She told herself many times that she couldn't just stop and look, no matter how curious she was. But she longed to spend some time in the shop with the long capes hanging out front. Or the one with the leather shoes lining a shelf just outside. Or even the one with the fine scarves.

Christine followed the road along, always choosing the wider road when it spread out, until finally, she found herself standing in front of what had to be the palace.

Slabs of slate covered the walls, black but with just a hint of iridescence. White stone blocks framed all the windows, which were made of leaded glass. The building was at least three stories tall, though Christine had the sense that it had more stories underneath, comfortable tunnels and chambers.

A bridge connected the street to the palace grounds. Christine's water sense let her know there was power there, enough to splash up and drown invaders crossing the bridge. It also told her that the water encircled the entire palace, like a moat.

With trepidation, Christine stepped onto the bridge. Would it recognize her? Throw her off? Send off an alarm?

But the bridge accepted her weight mutely. The stones of the bridge were ancient, colored a light brown. The path wasn't smooth, as if to honor the original shape of the rocks that made up the walkway.

The bridge itself was wide enough for a half-dozen trolls to parade across it, side by side. Wooden balustrades marched along the sides, the straight line broken up with tall wooden poles.

Would banners hang from those poles sometimes?

Criminals? Garlands of flowers? Christine could only imagine.

No one walked beside her as she crossed the bridge. It was probably only her imagination that the world seemed to be holding its breath.

Guards stood outside the door to the palace. They wore navy blue jackets and breeches, with thick black boots and peaked metal helmets. The two were broad and muscled, though only a bit taller than Christine. She could tell they were both exceptionally strong.

Scabbards holding curved swords were tied to their belts. Net bags full of sharp rocks hung there as well. That made sense to her—she could accurately throw any stone and hit whatever she aimed for.

Christine straightened herself all the way up so she could (almost) look them in the eyes.

"I am Princess Kizalynn Linumok Te'Dur," she announced. "Tell the king I've arrived."

The eyes of both guards widened tremendously, like Rodericket's had. They looked at each other, as if asking what they should do now. The one on the right gaped with shock.

Finally, the one on the left shook himself and addressed her in Trollish.

Christine sighed and shook her head. "I'm sorry, I was raised in the human realm. A changeling," she told them. "I don't understand you."

The guard nodded as he stepped to the side, then gestured at the door behind him. "Could you please place your left hand here?" he said in perfectly good English.

Christine blinked, surprised. There was a test? Of

course, there would be a test. Not for her in particular, but in case someone came to the palace who only pretended to be a troll.

A raised wooden oval filled the center of the door. A handprint had been carved into it.

Christine hesitated for a moment, asking her elements if they felt anything untoward. But none of them had ever experienced anything like this before.

Christine raised her left hand and gingerly set it against the wood.

It didn't surprise her when she suddenly found herself falling into the dark.

CHAPTER 11

Christine's fire element blazed all around her, lighting her way. She knew that while her body still stood on the threshold to the castle, her senses were here, deep under the palace.

She felt the strong stone bindings that had been placed on her senses. They would have stopped anyone who wasn't a troll, who didn't have a feel for stone and earth.

With just a flick of her wrists, the bindings fell away.

Simple enough test. She could go back to her body now.

But Christine wanted to do more. She wanted to make her announcement, finally.

She called up all her elements as her senses slowly floated back up to where her body stood.

Her air power pulled winds in, causing them to circle and dance around her motionless body. Her water element bubbled up, filling the space with joy. The stones under her feet trembled with her earth power, warming and singing with her fire element.

Christine found each and every one of the royal troll sigils buried deeply in the doors of the palace and brought those forth. The lopsided treble clefs filled with blue light and shone on the two guards.

The guards both stepped back. They'd probably never seen such a thing before.

Christine almost felt sorry for them, though she had warned them.

She was Princess Kizalynn. And she had returned.

~

The doors burst open after Christine stepped back. A richly dressed troll stood there, looking around in a panic. He wore a black, velvet tunic with a standing white collar. A necklace of large rubies went down past his chest. He also had rings on almost every finger.

The skin of his face was a softer green than Christine's, almost pale, though his hair was black and coarse, like hers. He had a smaller nose than the other trolls she'd seen, though she would bet he was forever sticking it into places where it didn't belong. His lower tusks were shorter as well, almost dainty compared to the two guards, though his upper tusks looked formidable. He smelled of pomegranates and caramel, a sickly sweet combination.

He shouted in Trollish. If Christine had to guess, she'd say he was asking who had done this, then demanding if it had been her.

She really wished there was an immersive language course she could take online so she could have at least the basics of Trollish by now!

Instead, she calmly smiled at him while she waited for him to run down. Only when he'd finally stopped ranting did she reply, "I am Princess Kizalynn Linumok Te'Dur. I have returned, but only for a short while."

The man blinked. Stepped back. Finally switched to English. "No. That's not possible! You were killed as a child. I saw to it myself!"

Christine reached out and grabbed the arm of the man before he could run away. "What did you just say?" Winds circled the man, pressing against him. Her earth power thrummed, increasing the strength of her grip.

The man froze. "Nothing, my lady."

"You lie," Christine said, her earth power hearing the truth, particularly since she had a good hold of him.

He *had* just said what she'd thought he'd said! That he was one of the ones responsible for her supposed death and who had celebrated her demise. Possibly, he'd benefited from it as well.

"That's Chamberlain McDommokin," one of the guards told her quietly.

She felt them standing solidly behind her. Seemed this chamberlain wasn't much liked. "Keep him well guarded while I go see the king," Christine told the guards. She didn't have time to deal with this chamberlain or even with the court politics.

"Aye, my lady," said the one on the right. He reached out with a silver binding chain, very similar to the ones Nik sold, and wrapped it around the chamberlain's wrists.

It was close to noon, she could tell. She expected there to be bells soon, ringing the time. (Did trolls have actual deities they worshipped? Beyond the good solid earth, clean water, fire and air?)

"I'll lead you," the other guard said, marching ahead of her and into the palace.

Christine took a deep breath. This was what she'd come to do, to root out the conspiracy that had left her presumed dead.

Time to go meet her uncle the king, and to find out if he was in on the plot as well.

⁓

Christine passed through galleries of finely painted scenes from the history of the trolls, probably important battles and treaties. She wished her phone was working so she could at least take some pictures so she could study them later.

The next long room appeared to be a formal dining hall, with long stout tables and merely benches, not chairs. Sage green walls made the place seem more comfy. Yet the place settings on the tables themselves had forks, knives, glasses, and fine red-and-gold plates.

She didn't have time to ask who ate there as they passed quickly into another long hallway.

The route seemed circuitous, until Christine realized that the guard was taking her the back way. They passed through the larger hallways quickly, avoiding anyone who might try to stop them, going in and out of rooms instead.

"What's your name?" Christine asked as they finally paused outside of another grand set of closed doors.

"Alberthendi," the guard replied. "At your service."

He knocked once, then threw the doors open before anyone responded. He led the way into what Christine quickly realized was the throne room.

As they marched, all the people grew silent. Christine longed to stop and study each and every one of them. They wore gorgeous clothing, velvets and silks. There were even a couple of women in gowns, though most of them wore long pants. Only the men favored breeches. Most of the colors were metallic, gold and silver, with different shades of browns and blacks.

Strange. Christine herself favored brighter jewel tones, particularly since the changeling spell had broken.

The room didn't have a high ceiling (as it shouldn't). While there were dim lights set in the corner, gems and precious stones, many about the size of her troll-fist, covered the ceiling and provided their own light. The room was longer than it was wide. Over two dozen trolls gathered in it comfortably.

A stone platform stretched across the front of the room. Christine found herself swallowing nervously as she approached.

She recognized the king when she saw him, from the visions her air power had brought her. He had the same green tint to his skin as she had. Long white hair poured out from underneath his heavy gold crown. He wore a plain black velvet tunic, sleeveless, that showed his muscles, as well as the scars running down his arms. Massive gold rings covered his fingers.

His tusks showed his true age, as they looked yellow and brittle. The top of his right ear had been lopped off—

probably in a battle long ago. He sat braced on his black onyx throne, as if prepared for the worst.

Christine stepped in front of the king, noting the lovely stone floors. Really, why did humans think wood was the best surface for anything? She looked around at the silent onlookers. Was she supposed to curtsey or something? She'd never been good at that sort of thing.

Instead, she bowed her head and announced, once again, "I am Princess Kizalynn Linumok Te'Dur. I was taken to the human plane as a baby and raised there. My powers were illegally taken from me, and bound. I have returned, but just for a short time. The Great War still looms."

The king slowly rose from his seat. At least he had the good sense to speak to her in English. "Are you really? Could you be? Hamin!"

Suddenly, the messenger from the court whom Christine had met before came pushing forward.

"It is her, my king," Hamin said proudly. "I told you she would come. You fixed the bridge?" Hamin asked, turning to her.

"I did. For now," Christine said. "There's a demon who's sworn to destroy it every time I rebuild it."

The king looked crestfallen. "So you can't stay?"

Christine, feeling full of daring, stepped up, onto the dais and toward the king. When he offered his hands, she took them, noting both how rough they felt as well as their strength.

"No, I cannot stay," she said, making sure that he'd hear the regret in her voice. "I need to go stop this demon.

Lars. I don't know if I can stop the Great War. But it might be my Destiny to fight in it."

The old king nodded and smiled. "You have your mother's eyes. And her courage. Yes, it is your Destiny. It was said that you'd be a great leader one day."

"I'd like to see my father," Christine said.

The king's look hardened. "Your father betrayed me," he said harshly, withdrawing his hands from hers.

"Like how Chamberlain McDommokin did?" Christine replied.

"What do you mean?" the king asked.

"The chamberlain is a traitor," the guard Alberthendi said as he stepped forward. "He was the one who saw to the death of Princess Kizalynn. He admitted it when he saw her."

"How is that possible? He was my closest advisor!" the king said, bewildered.

Without warning, Christine's air power rose and filled the room with winds. Her earth element set the rocks trembling beneath their feet. Fire danced from the stones in the ceiling, and the sound of rushing water was heard everywhere.

The king took another step back. "But how?" he said. "Very few trolls have so much power!"

Christine shrugged. She hadn't known that she was stronger than the average magical troll. Tina had always admired how much power Christine had. Christine had always assumed her elements were so strong because they'd had to "grow up" without her, constantly fighting and struggling to be free of their prisons. "You will tell me the truth," she announced, looking out over the trolls standing there. "Who helped the chamberlain?"

Two trolls stepped up, looking guilty. Alberthendi raised his hand, signaling the guards at the back of the room to come forward.

Christine didn't believe that they'd caught all the traitors. This kind of corruption went deep, and would take time to root out. But for now, she'd at least pulled a thorn from the king's side.

"Are you certain my father's a traitor?" Christine asked softly, turning her attention back to the king.

He gave her a calculating look. "Let's go see, shall we?" he said.

Christine's powers released the room, though it had been thrilling how every element there had responded to her. That, as much as anything else, reassured her that she was, indeed, royalty.

She followed the king out of a door behind the dais, her head held high. She didn't know if she'd be able to rescue her bio-dad. She was still going to try.

And then she was going to have a proper meal before she left.

~

Christine wished that she'd been wrong about the king, that he might have sentenced her bio-dad to house arrest or something.

No, he'd been placed in the dungeon. It was a horrible place. The stones here had been enspelled so that they brought only cold and no comfort. A long hallway ran the length of the dungeon, with cells dug into the rock on either side. Thick iron bars burned with cold fire to lock the prisoners away.

At least there weren't many prisoners here. Or maybe Trollville believed in capital punishment. She wasn't sure that made it any better.

"Obviously, only trolls are kept here," the king assured Christine. "Demons have their own dungeon. Humans, too."

How many humans or demons came into Trollville? What sorts of crimes did they commit that required them to be locked away? She had so much to learn! If only there was a guide book or something. Like the Lunar Planet Guide to Trollville.

Maybe she could write one later…

Christine had to be shown which cell held her bio-dad. She hadn't thought there was anyone in the dark, cavernous space, that it merely held a large pile of rags, about three feet high and across, bunched together to the right. On the left side stretched what looked like an uncomfortable cot, with no blankets or pillow. A small stream flowed at the very back of the cell—a cesspool for waste.

"Te'Dur," the king called. "Time to plead your innocence one last time."

The bundle of rags stirred.

Christine gasped as a troll rose up from the pile. He was tall, taller than the king. But the cell was too small, and he couldn't straighten up all the way. His hair was long, white, and stringy. Both of his tusks had been broken off. The shirt he wore had at one point been fine, but now was filthy and bore holes. Scars ran across the exposed skin of his arms and chest. His breeches were ragged around the bottoms and stained. He'd been curled up under what had probably at one point been blankets, but were now rags, at best.

"What is it?" Te'Dur roared. "Why do you disturb me? Take me away from sweet dreams?"

Christine blinked. Had being imprisoned for so long had affected her bio-dad's sanity?

"What were your dreams about?" Christine asked quietly.

Suddenly, Te'Dur smiled. His teeth looked painfully rotted. "I dreamed of you, child," he said softly. "Of your return." He shrugged. "Maybe this is all still a dream. But I heard you, deep underground. Touching the stones and making them sing."

"That was me," Christine said, guessing that he'd felt her calling the stones when she'd been tested by the entrance to the palace. "And I am here. You are not dreaming."

Te'Dur crouched back down again. "No, no, cruel demon. You are here to torment me. Again. After I proved my allegiance to the king, he still threw me down here."

Christine glared at the king, but he looked unrepentant. "Tell me, what did you do?" Christine said.

"After I saved you? Had you whisked away so that none could harm you? Letting those who wished you harm believe they had succeeded?"

"You mean like Chamberlain McDommokin?" Christine said.

The sly look surprised her. "Maybe. Maybe not."

"See?" the king said. "He won't tell me the names of his co-conspirators."

"He's probably afraid of retribution. Besides, if he tells you their names, then he's no longer useful and you'll kill him," Christine pointed out. That was just one of the reasons why torture had always seemed so stupid to her. Yes, you might escape the pain, but then you were just dead.

The king just crossed his arms across his chest and looked stubborn.

Christine turned back to Te'Dur. "We know that Chamberlain McDommokin is guilty. He thought he'd killed me."

Te'Dur looked at her, puzzled. "You can't be real," he said softly. "No, no, I need to continue sleeping. This is too nice a dream."

"What else is he accused of?" Christine asked the king. "Since he obviously didn't kill his daughter, and merely protected the other guilty parties in an effort to save his own life."

"Treason is a horrible crime," the king said, flustered. "His lands and titles have all been stripped. He's also guilty of being a stubborn bastard."

Christine couldn't help but smile at that. Of course, that would be a crime that probably ran in her family.

Te'Dur stood hunched over, looking from Christine to his brother. He still appeared to believe he was dreaming, but maybe he was starting to wake up.

"And what else?" Christine said, wanting to shake the king.

The king stepped forward, up to the bars. Te'Dur

stepped closer as well. The guards who'd accompanied them stirred restlessly. One pulled out her sword and stood ready to skewer Te'Dur if he tried to harm his brother.

"Did you kill your wife?" the king asked softly. "The lovely Lady Linumok?"

Christine felt a sudden lump in her throat. She'd been named after her bio-mum as well?

"Yes," Te'Dur hissed. He hung his head. "I let her believe her only daughter was dead. I should have taken her into my confidence. Should have let her know. But she couldn't have kept the secret. She had to seem heartbroken. Be heartbroken. For the plan to work."

Christine shot the king a triumphant smile. See? Her bio-dad wasn't a killer.

"And what about your son? Did you lead the demons to him so he could be ambushed?" the king asked, his voice hard as granite.

"I did not," Te'Dur said.

Christine felt he was telling the truth, but there was more to the story.

"What happened?" she asked.

"I didn't lead the demons away," Te'Dur admitted, shaking his head. "I could have stopped the attack. But I didn't." He looked up, glaring at the king. "You would have needed to know what I was doing out there, in the northern woods, if I had come to the rescue. You would have asked and pried and insisted and everything else, all my other plans, would have come to ruin."

Te'Dur turned away from the king and looked

beseechingly at Christine. "It was all for you. All the things I did. So that you could save us all."

Christine blinked, surprised. Her bio-dad wasn't going to take any responsibility for his actions? It was all going to be solidly placed on her?

She looked at the king, who looked back at her. His expression was unreadable, set in stone and just as impassive. He, also, was going to leave it up to her. Her bio-dad wasn't completely sane. And he wasn't completely guiltless, either.

What was she going to do?

CHAPTER 12

Christine paced in front of the cell that held Te'Dur while she tried to form some plan. Te'Dur had stepped back from the bars, patience developed over years showing in every inch of his stooped over stance.

The others who had accompanied them into the dungeon had mostly left, gone to spread the news of the prodigal daughter's return. A few guards remained; the king stubbornly stayed, as well as Hamin and a few people from the court whom Christine didn't know.

Unfortunately, her stomach kept interrupting her, reminding her that it was well past breakfast, as well as lunchtime, and that food needed to be coming soon.

Finally, Christine developed what she hoped were some viable options. She turned to the guard, Alberthendi. "I can't leave Te'Dur on his own, here," she told the guard. "He needs someone to look after him."

Alberthendi nodded solemnly. "It would be my honor

to give him a place at my table, a roof over his head, a hearth to warm his feet at."

Hamin smiled at her encouragingly. "I and my family would help as well."

The king shook his head. "No. If I let him go, you need to take him with you. I don't want him here in the city causing trouble."

"But how can I take care of him?" Christine asked. She didn't have the resources to set her bio-dad up in a good home on the human plane.

Though Tina would probably help, out of guilt. But Christine didn't feel comfortable going down that path. She couldn't take care of Te'Dur herself. She wouldn't promise that, not until after she'd dealt with Lars and the others.

"I don't want to leave the nether lands," Te'Dur suddenly announced. "I'll leave the city, and good riddance. But I don't want to live on the human plane," he pleaded with Christine. "Take me someplace else."

Christine sighed. She'd thought she'd found a solution already!

"How about I take you to the tollhouse, just this side of the bridge?" she asked. Would Rodericket take in Te'Dur? Could they work together? Doing whatever it was that a toll keeper did?

"That might work," the king said. "Rodericket is loyal, and won't be turned by the likes of you."

"But—never mind," Christine said. She knew she'd never convince the king that her bio-dad was innocent. Particularly since he, himself, carried so much guilt over this deeds. "Free him. Release him into my care. After a shower and a meal, we'll get going."

"But, but why? Why must you leave so soon?" the king asked as he waved the guards forward.

The lock on the cell had both a physical and a magical component to it. Christine really wanted to see how it worked, but she forced herself to pay attention to the king instead.

Maybe Nik could tell her. If Nik wasn't arrested, or under protective custody, or something.

"I have to go back to the human plane to stop the demon Lars Sorgenfrey from destroying the bridge," Christine said. "Or to rebuild the bridge if he does break it again."

And somehow, to stop the Great War, though she wasn't sure how she was going to do that. Or was she supposed to let the war start, and she would just fight in it and help her side win?

Seriously. Why couldn't a Destiny be straightforward and spoken in plain language for once?

Te'Dur stepped out of his cell. With a loud sigh of relief, he straightened his back and stood all the way up.

He certainly was tall. Christine would have to find out if the Lady Linumok had been tall as well, or if her own height just came from him.

Te'Dur waved a hand over his rags, but nothing happened. "Too many spell-dampening rocks," he muttered. He still seemed to be in a daze, looking around as if trying to remember all the details of a really good dream.

"We still need a bath and a tailor," Christine told the king. "And maybe a meal."

The king studied Christine for a moment. "It's been a day or more since you've eaten, I'd bet," the king said, giving her a wide grin. "Come. Rouse the chefs. Let us prepare you a royal feast before sending you on your way."

Then he paused. For a moment, he seemed to deflate. "You will come back again, won't you? You are one of my few remaining heirs."

Christine beamed at him and said the words. "I will return. I promise."

She was happy to hear her words echo deep in the earth beneath her feet, indicating just how serious she was. The king seemed surprised, but then he gave her a great smile.

She would not be forsworn.

Christine didn't know how she was going to move. She was stuffed to her very eyeballs, and then some. Who knew that troll cooking was so delicious? She'd really been missing out.

Of course, they wouldn't have something handy like a cookbook she could take with her or anything…

But it was getting late. Afternoon shadows were already growing long. She needed to leave Trollville, get back to the gate, and see if the bridge was still extant, or if she would have to rebuild it again.

Hamin had sat at her right, explaining the dishes quietly, translating when people slipped into Trollish, and generally acting as her guide. She'd barely gotten to know him, but she knew that she'd miss him. Te'Dur sat on the other side of Hamin. He looked a changed man with his hair cut short and in clean clothes.

Christine still worried about the dazed look in his eyes. Hopefully more good food, and a good night's sleep, would help him find his equilibrium. Though she suspected that it would take a long time before he was fully recovered. Maybe even longer before he stopped looking around suspiciously, as if one of the nearby guards would suddenly lock him away again.

Christine talked a little with the king, who sat on her left, asking about Trollville, the Great War, were they well stocked for siege, would there be more travel to the human plane now that the bridge was open again.

She told him of rebuilding the bridge, how she'd tried to put truth into the stones so that oath breakers couldn't cross. The king didn't seem surprised at that, telling her that they had similar spells in different parts of the palace.

Finally, Christine told the king that it was time for her to leave.

The king nodded, stood, and clapped his hands, getting the entire table's attention. At least eighteen trolls had been at the feast, though Christine would be embarrassed trying to remember any of their names.

"It is time for Princess Kizalynn to be on her way, with our blessing. Let none hinder her steps, so that she might complete her great deeds and then return home."

The other trolls raised their glasses of sweet (sweet!) mead and said, "Hear! Hear!"

Christine was about to push her chair back when

Hamin placed his hand on her arm, indicating she should wait.

What now? She had to get going.

Three servants came in. The first carried what looked like a bolt of beautiful cloth. The second bore black boots. The third held a smallish sword.

"A great cloak of our people," the king announced.

Hamin now motioned for Christine to get out of her chair.

The cloak was heavily embroidered in gold and silver, with tiny precious stones embedded in the design. It looked like patchwork, almost, with smaller squares of cloth up top and longer rectangles below.

Christine gasped as the servant laid the cloak across her arms. It was heavily enchanted. What did it do?

Her air power levitated the cloak and shook it once, unfurling it. Then it floated down nicely, perfectly fitting around her neck.

She had the sense that this cloak would take care of her in the coldest of winters, as well as deflect most blades.

The black boots the next servant held slid easily onto her feet. They were also the exact right size. They felt better than any shoes she'd ever tried on before. The soles were thin and flat, allowing her to really feel the earth and draw up its power. They were warm and she'd bet, waterproof.

Christine accepted the dagger and tied it around her waist with the silver belt the king had provided, though she had no idea what the hell she was going to do with it. She'd never trained with a knife or sword.

One more thing to add to the list of things to learn.

"Thank you," Christine said simply. "It means more than I can say."

The king beamed at her. "You're welcome. May your journey be swift and your return even quicker."

He didn't say anything to Te'Dur, didn't even look at his brother.

"Come on, we've got a long way to go and not a lot of time," she told Te'Dur as they finally left the palace.

Te'Dur stopped for a moment just past the palace doors. He turned his face up toward the sky.

"I'm here," he said softly. "This is real."

Christine reached out her hand. "You have been freed from prison," she told him. "You have air to breathe."

Te'Dur took a deep breath, followed by another.

"Thank you," he said. "I dreamed of you coming. I never expected it to be real."

"We have to go quickly, now," Christine warned. "Though we'll stop when you need to."

Te'Dur nodded. "I'll make it," he told her grimly. "I will follow you to the ends of the earth and back without stop."

She nodded. He'd never ask for a break, but instead, would walk himself to death first. "We'll get there," she said. "I may have a plan."

"Really?" he asked. It sounded as though he was teasing her. For the first time, he gave her what felt like a warm smile. "I would expect nothing less."

Christine shook her head, then led the way back through Trollville. She was rarely that organized.

She just hoped he'd agree to her crazy idea.

Seemed that Christine's air power didn't like pushing other people around. It was happy to help Christine get places quickly. But her bio-dad? Not so much.

"But how do you balance on that little wheel?" Te'Dur asked, his head tilted to one side, confusion written all over his face.

"I'm not," Christine explained. Again. "The wheel is just an illusion. It helps me focus on where I want to go. I could travel without it."

"And why should I try this?" Te'Dur said. "Just to go fast?"

"Yes," Christine said. At least he finally appeared to be catching on to why she wanted to use her little wheel. "We need to get back to the toll bridge. Quickly."

"Why don't you just leap and race?" Te'Dur finally asked. "I remember. I used to be able to do that."

Christine gestured toward the open road. "Show me."

It was already twilight. It would be at least a few hours before they'd reach the bridge, even traveling at magical speeds.

Te'Dur nodded. He put one foot out in front of the other, as if he was getting ready for a race. Then he changed his feet. He paused, thinking, before changing his feet around again. "Sorry," he said after a few moments. "It's just that I haven't done this for so long. But I think it went like this."

Te'Dur swung his leg forward and took one great leaping bound.

Christine was not impressed.

But then he took a second. And a third. His strides got smoother, longer. With half a dozen steps, he soon reached a quarter-mile down the road.

Christine quickly asked her elements to power her along, imagining the little humming wheel between her feet.

Her bio-dad stopped and watched her come racing up before he turned and took off again.

It turned out that he could speed himself along as fast as she did. Was he really leaping that far? Or was it mostly his magic? And how long could he maintain it?

Christine kept looking over at him, worried. However, Te'Dur seemed to be having the time of his life. He laughed, throwing his head back and chortling gleefully. He seemed so alive like this, and nothing like that shambling mound she'd seen back in the prison cell.

But still, she slowed the moment she thought his energy started dragging. Fortunately, they'd covered almost the entire valley. Now, it was time to go up the hills, and into the mountains.

"Thank you," Te'Dur said again. "I know, I know," he said, holding his hands up to stop her from telling him yet again that she hadn't done that much. "You can't imagine how wonderful it is to finally be able to move freely. To lift my face up to the sky and laugh. To move quickly, effortlessly. I used to be the strongest troll in the guard." He shook his head. "But I cannot have more regrets than I already have. I have had the best gift of all today, a day of freedom. Thank you, daughter."

"I'm hoping there will be many more," Christine told him.

Te'Dur nodded, though he looked sad. "I cannot hope for more than I have already received," he said. "But come. We've rested enough."

"Okay," Christine said, letting him lead the way and set the pace.

"So tell me about Trollville," Christine said after they'd climbed a little way. The path had narrowed and they walked single file up the well-worn rocks. "Shouldn't there be, well, more color there?" It had bothered her more than she could say that everyone merely wore shades of metallic and not the bright jewel tones she loved.

Te'Dur barked a laugh. "You have the stupid chamberlain to thank for that. He swore those colors were more sophisticated. You've seen the market, right? Colors to rival the rainbow."

Christine sighed. No, she hadn't seen the market. But she would. Someday.

"What will happen to the chamberlain? And the others who conspired with him?" she asked next.

"Hopefully he gets put into my cell," Te'Dur growled. "But honestly, who can say? That man had power. And he hoped that his children would be next in line for the throne."

"Am I really an heir to the throne?" Christine asked.

Te'Dur nodded. "Yes, though I'm not sure of the order now. You had a prior claim to the boy the king's got lined up now, but you weren't here." He paused, then added, "And I'm sorry, but you probably aren't trollish enough."

Christine merely shrugged at that. "I know I need to learn to speak the language," she said. "And it will take me some time to understand the politics as well. But I think

I'm awfully trollish," she added. "I'm much more gruff than the humans I know."

That made Te'Dur smile at her over his shoulder. "That somehow doesn't surprise me, that your true troll nature always shone through."

He paused, then said, "Were they good to you? The humans?"

"Oh, yes!" Christine said. She told him of Mum and Dad, and her brother Dennis, and how they'd all worked to accept her even though she was a troll.

Te'Dur just shook his head. "I don't know if a troll family would have been so forgiving."

Christine had no answer for that.

She told him all about her past, how she'd been used as bait for Tina, who'd been told she had a Destiny. How the demons had kidnapped Tina in order to twist and pervert her Destiny, and how they all wanted to start the Great War.

"Do they really want a war? Those demons?" Te'Dur asked after being quiet for a while.

Christine wondered if he still needed to digest some of what she'd been telling him.

"Or is it more advantageous to them to build fear and doubt, and have the world always feeling as if it is on the brink of all-out war? To keep people afraid, and living on that fear?"

Christine blinked, surprised. That was actually a very astute question. "I think they want the war," she replied slowly. "However, I believe that they won't start it until they are certain they can win it. They mainly want to win the war, to be ascendant over all the races. Not to have a long protracted set of battles."

Te'Dur grunted at that. They'd reached a steeper part of the climb, and though Te'Dur would deny it, he was quickly growing winded.

How close were the demons to starting the war? Christine felt as though they were closer than they had been. What would prompt them to actually declare war, as opposed to having numerous skirmishes, as they had been doing?

Christine didn't know, but she was very afraid that she might find out soon.

Evening had set into the hills. The pines formed sharp shapes just off the trail. Though Christine could see well enough in the dark to find her way, things not directly in front of her were indistinct. The scent of a warm fire drifted on the breeze, along with the clean smell of the mountain rocks.

Christine would bet that while on the one hand, Te'Dur was pushing himself past exhaustion, on the other, the mountain air was healing him just as fast, the pure rocks a balm to his soul.

Rodericket had been waiting for them, it seemed. As soon as they crested the last hill, he popped up. "You're here! You're here!"

Christine had stopped short at that. "Is anyone waiting for us at the tollhouse?" she asked, her general paranoia getting the better of her.

Then again, she was dealing with demons. Could she be too paranoid?

"No, my lady!" Rodericket said, seeming to be shocked at such a question. "No one can oust me from my proper position. You'll see." Then he paused, looking significantly at Te'Dur.

"Rodericket, may I present Te'Dur," Christine said as formally as she could. She wasn't sure if she could still call Te'Dur a lord or not. She was going to have to ask him privately, later.

"It is an honor. An honor!" Rodericket said, bowing deeply.

Te'Dur nodded in return. Christine suspected if he tried to bow he'd fall over, exhausted.

"Come, let me provide you with all the comforts of home," Rodericket said, leading the way up the path to the tollhouse. "I've always believed in your innocence," he added over his shoulder.

Christine thought she detected a faint magical glow around the tollhouse as they drew closer. "What is that?" she asked, stopping. She wasn't going anywhere near someplace magical until she had an explanation.

Rodericket smiled at her. "It's my protection. I've worked at the tollhouse all my life, as did my da before me. This place is tuned to me and none other. The longer I live here, the stronger my position gets."

Huh. So maybe the protection charms that Christine had placed in the living room were stronger than they'd been when she'd first placed them. She'd have to ask Nik.

But first, she had to get to Nik.

As Rodericket walked forward in front of them, the

faint auburn glow around the house faded. It disappeared completely when Rodericket touched the door.

"Oh, my. Company! More company!" he said. He held the door open for Christine and Te'Dur. "Come in, come in! Need to get everyone settled."

Christine noted that the toll keeper hadn't just been waiting and watching for them. He'd been very busy cleaning, as well. Instead of looking like an abandoned waiting area at a train station, the waiting room had been spiffed up. Fresh flowers and sticks of baby pine with pinecone buds on them sat in vases on every table. The tablecloths had all been washed, the cobwebs wiped away, and all the lights fixed. The stone floor had been polished and was very comforting. A fire blazed in the huge hearth to her left.

Te'Dur looked around with satisfaction. "This might do quite nicely," he said. He walked over to a chair beside the fireplace and settled down heavily into it.

Rodericket was talking to beings—trolls, she'd bet—at the other door, the one closest to the bridge. She breathed a sigh of relief. Good. That meant the fairy bridge still stood.

For now.

Feeling very forward, Christine walked into the other part of the room, the half that had been carved out of the mountain. She quickly found a set of water pitchers filled to the brim with fresh spring water, along with flagons of all sizes. She poured herself one, drank it, drank a second, then finally poured a larger mug for Te'Dur and carried it out to him, bringing the pitcher of water as well.

"Thank you, my dear," Te'Dur said. He immediately

drank as much as she did. "That hits the spot." He shook his head.

Christine could tell the memories of prison had just risen up again.

Te'Dur sat for a moment looking at his mug before he took another sip. "Mighty fine," was all he said, though his voice sounded as though it was coming from far away.

Rodericket finally allowed the large group of trolls into the waiting room. "Now, you don't have to make a decision right now. There's places to rest around back, if you want to wait until morning. In the meantime, sit, have some water, I'll bring the stew out in a jiff."

He turned to Christine, surprised. "You found the water yourself? You should have waited! It would have been my pleasure to serve you. An honor!"

Christine smiled at the flustered toll keeper. "I did see to myself. And to Te'Dur. Please see that he has a good helping of stew before he sleeps, though I'm afraid you may have to wake him to get him to eat."

Rodericket peered past her. While Te'Dur still had his eyes open, he was starting to droop. He'd had more physical activity in that one day than he'd had in several years.

"Be gentle with him," she told Rodericket quietly. "He's precious to me." She had no other word for it. He was still a stranger, with a rough past, but she'd grown to respect him this past day. Plus, she really wanted the opportunity to get to know him better, and find out more of their family history. Maybe he'd even be willing to teach her Trollish.

"I will, My Lady," Rodericket said. "Now, you need to

be getting back. This family came through without injury, but they also raced across the bridge, feeling like shadowy demons were chasing them."

Christine had never gotten the knack of raising just one eyebrow. She still tried while she said, "We'll see about that." She paused, then bowed low to Rodericket. "Thank you for your aid and your comfort, toll keeper." She wished she could have said something about rewarding him well for his efforts, but she honestly didn't know much about the money system here.

"It is my honor and privilege," Rodericket said.

Christine whirled, her cloak twirling dramatically, then walked to the door back to the bridge. The troll family shrank back and gasped. As she closed the door behind her she heard them asking about royalty.

Yes, she was a troll princess. She'd certainly been feted as one by the king, who would have thrown a week-long series of balls and parties if she'd been staying.

Maybe another time.

She'd done what she'd planned on doing. Gone to see Trollville, to talk to the king, to free her bio-dad.

Now she just had to prevent the Great War and save the world.

How hard could that be?

CHAPTER 13

Christine hurried up the mountain path past the tollhouse, hoping she wasn't too late to stop that idiot Lars from destroying the bridge a second time.

Okay, so technically her ex-boyfriend Joe had destroyed the bridge. But he'd only done it at Lars' bidding.

She knew that wouldn't stand up in the court of the Host, however. They would take demon influence into account when it came to humans. But it was difficult to magically influence *kith and kin*. They needed logic and words instead. Many of the races knew quickly when someone lied.

Though honestly, she already knew from experience that almost any time a demon spoke, they were lying.

What had happened to Joe? Was he just so angry about the pair of them falling apart that he wanted to destroy the work she did?

Or was it something darker? Did Lars have some

blackmail material? Joe had always told her that he had a checkered past, and had been kicked out of Trollville.

She recognized the bridge instantly. It looked identical to the bridge she'd rebuilt. The far end of it seemed hazy, though, even in the dim light.

Was that magic? Or more stupid snow?

Christine wrapped her cloak more firmly around her. She realized now that the cloak was armored. Between the outer layer and inner lining hung a light sheet of magical chainmail. She wondered if it was like that mythical Elven armor that was so popular now from the movies (though still stupid-looking, at least on humans).

She even drew the dagger from her belt, holding it in her right hand. Huh. It didn't feel as awkward as she'd been afraid it would. Perhaps that was because the haft had been deliberately built for a troll hand.

Maybe there were some YouTube videos she could watch about knife fighting. Just one more thing for her to learn.

Christine paused and bowed her head at the edge of the bridge before setting a foot on the stones. She'd never been one for prayers. Since meeting actual angels and devils, she had even further questions about God and Satan and whether such beings existed (since no one admitted to ever seeing them) or if they were really just powerful beings and not gods at all.

However, being here had made her feel so much more connected to all her innate powers, as well as to the natural elements. She thanked them for helping her, and asked them politely for their aid in the coming battle.

Her own elements surged around her, the fire lighting

her way, winds swirling her hair, earth pushing up at her feet, and the water stirring her blood.

Here goes nothing, was all she could think of.

Then she *charged* across the bridge.

S now howled past Christine's eyes as she came into the human plane. Her face felt instantly frozen, though the cloak protected her way better than any jacket. She couldn't see anything but whiteness until her air element pushed the snow away.

The stench of demons remained in the air, despite the strong winds blowing. Christine sensed more than saw a shadow demon directly in front of her, at the end of the bridge.

She lunged with the dagger, then nearly dropped it when it landed a solid blow. The demon she'd hit screamed with rage.

Interesting. Christine didn't know how to fight with a dagger or any sort of blade, but she still did her best to slash at the beasts who drew close enough for her to strike.

There were still too many of them. Her cloak now defended her from their side attacks, though. She wished she could see them better.

Her fire element heard her plea and outlined the pack.

Christine swallowed hard. Okay, maybe it wasn't so good to see them. There were so many! Why were they here? Were they about to raid Trollville?

It took her a moment to realize that the demons were all in front of her. Not one of them had circled around her. They didn't take more than a step or so onto the bridge.

She took a deliberate step back, backing up onto the bridge, out of reach of the demons.

They stayed where they were, growling and trying to slash out at her.

When she moved forward, they attacked again.

Were they trying to hold her here? Make sure she didn't escape?

Christine took a step backwards, onto the bridge. Then another. Then another.

The snarling pack of shadow demons lit by her fire element stayed at the edge of the bridge.

She couldn't go forward. She couldn't go backwards.

She was damned tired, though, of being stuck in limbo.

"All right, Lars, you've had your fun," Christine called out. "When's the real party going to start?"

Lars suddenly appeared in the center of the shadow demons. Or was that just an apparition of him? She wasn't sure, given how the shadow demons appeared to fade in and out around him.

He wore a plain white shirt with a casual dinner jacket over it, as if the cold were beneath him. A sword grew in his hands.

Crap. A huge, flaming sword that made the dagger in Christine's hands look like a toothpick in comparison.

"The real party?" Lars asked. "Right now."

Christine dodged another swinging blow from Lars. He was so fast! And he had a much greater reach than she did. She kept his attention on her while her elements amassed yet another attack of rocks, finding large boulders for her this time.

She was still proud of the cut on Lars' face from her first attack. The magical shield he had around him effectively blocked all her magical attacks, but not her physical ones.

He hadn't been expecting her to dump half a yard of gravel, rocks, and ice on him from above. Trolls were known for keeping their word, as well as for being straightforward and honest. Had he really not realized that her people could be sneaky as well?

She just needed to keep his attention on her while her powers brought a few more rocks into reach…

Lars' sword cut through the air in front of her with a loud roar. That damned weapon of his had a mind of its own.

However, Lars, like the humans, insisted on asserting his dominance over his tools and the elements.

Christine had learned her lesson, and tried to stay out of the way while her own elements did the real work. She was the decoy, here.

She poked at his shield with her dagger, but it couldn't get through. While her own weapon was physical, it had too much magic in it, so Lars' shield deflected it.

Her attempts continued to distract him. He gave her a smug smile and knocked her hand to the side with a hard blow.

Ow.

The dagger went flying over the edge of the bridge.

Christine let it lay in the snow. Her air element would fetch it soon enough.

"More rocks? Gravel?" Lars sneered. He pushed forward another step, driving Christine back.

She threw a string of lights at him, mostly to confuse him.

The gaily colored lights actually penetrated the shield. They were magical, but they couldn't cause any harm. He spent an amusing moment slashing at the lights dancing around his face.

Large boulders, each about half a man tall, rose up behind Lars while he wasn't paying attention. More raced at him from the front.

Lars suddenly realized that he was surrounded. "How dumb do you think I am? Those can't hold me a third time."

Christine nodded and waited a few seconds while the rocks joined together, forming a solid circle around him. Another rock floated over his head.

Lars could escape. But he'd have to kneel down to slide under the rocks.

Christine knew that he'd be too proud to get on his knees in front of her.

The rocks didn't stop him from moving. They also didn't try to block his magic. They were there to hem him in for a while and make him stand still.

"See?" he smirked at her as he waved his arms. "Not working." Though he couldn't actually get a good swing in with his sword, now.

"Yes, it is," Christine said as her air element returned her dagger to her hand. She pointed her weapon at him. "You are standing on *my* bridge. The bridge that I have built. This bridge denies all oath breakers. You can only remain here if you change into your natural state."

Christine took a deep breath, then let it out. "Transform," she commanded.

"You can't make me," Lars said, as smugly as any teenager. He abruptly shivered. A look of worry crossed his face. "What the—"

"Transform," Christine intoned again.

Lars' shoulder lifted, its dimensions changing. He forced it back down. "No!" he screamed. "You can't do this to me!"

"Transform," Christine told him a third time.

Lars' other shoulder jerked back. Wings made of torn black leather with struts of bone started to erupt.

"I can't!" Lars said, starting to sound panicked.

He sounded like a three year old complaining about being sent to bed.

His chest pushed forward, ripping his oh-so-nice shirt. Not that Christine was happy about Lars ruining his clothing. Really.

Lars roared as his legs shot up, expanding suddenly into their natural length. He stayed bent over, pressed against the rock above his head that was holding him in. His face grew long and more like a ram's skull.

With a strangled scream, Lars pushed himself up. The rocks hemming him in broke apart, the stone that had been above his head flying.

Christine let them all fall away.

A huge demon rose up above her, as tall as a two story building. He seemed part snake, part ram, and part great dragon. Shimmering yellow-tinted scales covered his long torso, looking sickly and poisoned. Powerful legs crouched underneath him, scaled in a white and black pattern. In one hand, he still held the huge flaming sword. It looked small for him, now. His great wings flapped, swirling the snow around him.

Could this idiot breathe fire? Christine ducked down as he roared. The sound vibrated in her chest, deep and low.

Great fangs stuck out from his upper snout. The rest of his teeth weren't very pretty either, and black poison dripped from his long, forked tongue.

Christine couldn't help her shiver when Lars focused his great black eyes on her. They were soulless pits that would eat her alive given the chance.

"Time to die now, troll," Lars said in his booming voice.

Christine deliberately rolled her eyes at him. "Oh, please. Can't you come up with anything original to say? You've told me that before. But you haven't managed to kill me yet."

Lars stopped for a moment. Blinked.

Ugh. Did his eyelids really need to look like tattered and flayed skin? Gross.

"You are correct," he told her. He thought for a moment, then shrugged.

"No matter. I will kill you, then come up with something pithy to say for the history books."

Before Christine could reply, Lars roared again and reached down with his bare hand, trying to claw her.

Christine dodged instead of attacked. She had to make the fight look real, though in actually, she was just playing a waiting game.

It was illegal for Lars to transform into his demon self here on the human plane.

Where was the Host? Why hadn't they come to grab him yet? It *was* late on a Tuesday night, but surely someone was still awake?

How could Christine call them? Make them come and do their duty? Capture this defiant demon?

She tried slashing at his powerful legs, but her dagger glanced off the scales.

They'd come. She just had to delay Lars for a little while longer.

If they didn't…there wouldn't be a princess who needed saving anymore.

Christine mourned the rips in her brand-new cloak. Though she'd rather sacrifice it than her own skin.

Lars' claws were nasty. And poisoned, she bet.

Her boulders were ineffective against him, no matter how many landed a solid blow. For a while, she'd wondered if he was really there, if this was just an apparition she fought. However, she had managed to strike him. Once. And it had been a solid, real blow.

Her air power had at least tamed his stupid wings. He couldn't use those at all, not without getting blasted with winds that would throw him off balance. So he kept his wings tucked in close to his body.

Her fire element seemed to delight him, as if he could draw energy from it. Water had proved more effective, especially when turned into ice, but she still wasn't strong enough to hold him.

Damn it! Where was the Host? Why hadn't they shown up yet?

The shadow demons massed underneath the bridge, howling up at her. They couldn't attack her up here. She'd assumed it was because they were all oath breakers.

She glanced over her right shoulder. She clearly saw the tollhouse and the trail to Trollville. Would Lars go there next, if he killed her? Would he lead the army of shadow demons in an attack if she left the bridge undefended?

All those innocent, good trolls. They'd fight, and die.

No.

Lars couldn't win.

But how could she get the Host to pay attention to the fact that a demon had transformed into his natural form here on the human plane?

Christine continued to fight back. When the next swing of Lars' sword went whooshing by, she tried to hit his arm as it passed.

Only to find herself knocked on her ass. Again.

He just moved so fast! He was going to knock her clear off the bridge, next.

Christine rolled to the side and scrambled to her feet, dodging the next attack.

Wait a moment.

Why hadn't he knocked her off the side? Or pushed her back to the far end of the bridge?

The bridge—like all bridges—was neither here or there. They existed between things, between earth and sky, between Trollville and Earth, between the planes of *kith and kin* and the human plane.

No wonder the Host hadn't arrived! They didn't know Lars had transformed, as he'd oh-so-carefully stayed on the bridge while he'd been attacking her.

Christine dodged another blow, letting her momentum take her to the human side of the bridge, resting for a moment against the strong stone balustrade.

Leaping over the side of the bridge would put her in the center of a pack of shadow demons.

But she had to get out of here. She couldn't turn and run away—Lars moved too damned quickly for that. He'd stop her before she got to the far end.

Oh well.

Out of the frying pan and into the fire.

While Lars recovered from his next swing, she leaped off the bridge and into the chaos below.

Christine howled as the shadow demons attacked. She regretted taking the deep breath as soon as she did, though, because the stench seared her lungs.

Her arms were on fire from claw wounds. Her cloak had been ripped to shreds. It had given up its life protecting her. Her water element worked on any demon Christine did manage to strike, causing the demon's icky blood to bubble up, bleeding it to death quickly, even for minor wounds.

Fire didn't have any effect on the stupid shadow demons, though her fire element did light them up for her to see, so they couldn't sneak up on her. Her earth element couldn't do much, as rocks tended to sail right through them. Ice helped, and sometimes winds could knock the demons aside.

Mostly, though the demons stayed in their shadowy plane and would only physically manifest a paw full of claws, or a snout full of jagged teeth, while the rest of them stayed away.

Christine panted and tried to move out from the center of the pack. Lars had stayed on top of the bridge. She didn't look up, afraid that she'd get too angry if he was laughing at her. She had to get him to come down *here*, while still in his demon form.

But how?

Her earth element got lucky with a couple of rocks, clearing a brief path for Christine. She lunged that way, then continued to take one painful step at a time, directing the mass of shadow demons away from the bridge.

Snow whirled around her, freezing the parts of her that weren't burning from the demons' poison. She still heard Lars' booming laugh as she fought, step by step.

"You know, I don't have to kill you myself," Lars drawled. "I can just let my minions do it for me."

Christine didn't pause in her struggle, though her earth power was starting to drain. She just needed a brief rest to regain her strength.

The demons weren't pausing at all.

"Why let them have all the fun?" Christine finally managed. All those movies, or hell, even the books, that had heroes making blithe comments while in the middle of a raging battle were just *wrong*.

When Lars didn't answer, Christine said, "You'd lose all bragging rights, you know." Lars still didn't reply. Christine finally risked a look up. The stupid demon stood tall and proud, as if it owned the bridge.

Her bridge.

It just wasn't right. She had to get him off of there, right now.

"I suppose I could just let them wear you down, then deal the final blow," Lars finally said.

That gave Christine's tired brain an idea. She had to act hurt, enough so that he'd think she was no longer a threat. So she screamed loudly the next demon claws raked her arm, as if she'd been mightily wounded.

She remembered the conversation she'd had with Te'Dur. The demons would only start the Great War once they were convinced they could win it.

She had to convince Lars that he could win. She screamed again, this time in real pain. She slowed her defense and panted.

Damn it! How weak did she have to be before he'd come and "finish her off" as he claimed he would?

She roared and tried to escape the pack of howling shadow demons, something she'd never done before. They massed closer to her now, hemming her in.

Everything hurt. Her arms. Her legs. Her back. Her stomach. Even her feet.

She swung and missed with her dagger, almost falling over with the momentum.

Crap. She really was hurt and injured. And yes, okay, dying.

Another blow from a demon made her whirl the other way, unable to stop herself.

No. She would not die like this.

Everything slowed down, like it did in the movies. Her little dagger felt too heavy to lift, but she still heaved it up trying to defend herself from the next blow. She panted, shaking her head, trying to get rid of the sudden sweat from her eyes.

A thump that shook the earth beside her startled her. She found herself falling. She had to get back up. Had to rise. Had to fight.

But she felt so tired. All she wanted to do was sleep. Rest on the solid earth.

Recover.

Demon laughter surrounded her.

"Such a pretty troll. Finally found your proper place, down on the ground, underneath my feet," Lars sneered. He reached out with one great clawed foot and pressed down on one of Christine's legs.

She howled with pain as the bone snapped.

"You cannot escape your true fate, to be ruled by my kind."

Christine finally opened her eyes. She continued to lie there and pant, making herself cringe from the sight in front of her.

Lars was pretty ugly, so it wasn't that difficult.

She couldn't show him how the earth gave her

strength. Her earth power continued to seep into her, building her back up. She'd only needed a moment or two of respite to start healing from her wounds. Something she was pretty sure Lars didn't realize.

"You are merely the first," Lars said smugly. "Soon, all your people will be ruled by us."

Christine didn't laugh in his face, though she was tempted to. She didn't bother telling him that she'd already gotten rid of the Chamberlain. Certainly there would be more corrupt trolls in the court, but the king had time to ferret them out, now that the Chamberlain wasn't whispering treason in his ear.

"You can't kill me," Christine panted up at him. "I'm a princess!"

She felt a slight tremor deep in the earth beneath her. She took a deep breath and called out, "I am Princess Kizalynn Linumok Te'Dur, heir to the throne of Trollville. You are merely a demon. I do not answer to you."

Lars sneered at her. He didn't feel the earth start to ring, a deep, somber tone.

"Princess or not, you'll soon be dead," Lars said. He raised his great sword over his head. "Prepare your soul for Hell," he intoned.

A great booming voice echoed in the clearing. "Lars Sorgenfrey, you have broken the terms of your parole by transforming into your true demon shape while on the earthly plane. Prepare to be judged."

"No!" Lars screamed.

He suddenly slashed down with his sword.

Rocks that Christine's earth power brought up to

block the blow shattered. Christine rolled to the side, screaming mightily when the sword sliced her arm.

Cold. So cold.

Christine was only vaguely aware when a troop of angels arrived. The light spilling out from them caused the shadow demons to flee into the darkness. Lars shrank back down, abruptly changing from his demon form to human size. The smell of sulfur and rotten cabbage was replaced with the sweet smell of jasmine.

Christine's earth element pushed as much power into her as it could. Her water element doused her arm with chilling water carried there by the air. Her fire element burned hot in her belly, trying to chase away the cold that crept toward her heart.

An angel bent down beside Christine. It looked kind of male. Christine couldn't help her shivers, though. Damned things were just so disturbing, like a wax doll animated by a creepy spell. Nothing natural was that perfect.

The angel waved its hand over her leg, healing the break there. Then it pulled away the cold seeping into her.

"You are now strong enough to go to court," it proclaimed.

What the hell? Christine still felt completely exhausted and torn up. Her stomach growled. She needed food and rest. She was *so* not up to making an appearance at the court of the Host.

She had no choice. A gold oval swirled around her, lessening the hold of the earth on her.

"Be right back," she promised the bridge as the whirlwind sent by the court took her away.

CHAPTER 14

C hristine lay on the cold linoleum of the hallway outside one of the courtrooms.

Ugh.

She hurt *everywhere.*

She hadn't noticed before how being in the courthouse delicately bound her elements, making them quiet down. That also meant they couldn't help her.

She turned her head. Yuck. The gray linoleum, underneath the scuffed wooden board along the bottom of the wall, was cracked and yellowing along the edges. Maybe she was still smelling things from the battle, but she sure caught a whiff of smelly demon down here.

Christine forced herself to sit up. At least no one was there to watch her. She pulled herself together as best she could. She gave herself a fresh white tunic that hung down to mid-thigh, along with brown breeches and black ankle boots. She hid her injured arm, conjuring up a sling.

Hopefully she didn't look too much of a mess. She

knew that some races could see past her disguise, but at least she'd made the effort.

She pushed herself up to her feet. Her recently broken leg ached. She felt fragile, and only put weight on it gingerly.

The door to the courtroom swung slowly as she pushed at it. She had to put far too much effort into opening it. Was she that weak?

This courtroom looked different than the others she'd been in. The judge sat on the left side of the room, by himself, without any advisors sitting beside him. The judge's bench looked more like a huge wooden pulpit carved out of black wood. She'd bet it was octagonal, though she couldn't see the back in order to count the flat sides.

Directly in front of her sat a large collection of the Host, both angels and demons. The demons were in their true form, some of them large enough to take up two or three seats. The angels sat primly but were no less disturbing, what with the bright light they constantly shed and their huge wings.

Was this a jury trial? She'd never been to one of those.

Opposite the judge was a second pulpit, made out of the same dark wood, though not as grand. Would that be where witnesses would testify?

The rest of the room looked the same as the other courtrooms she'd been in, with two tables up front, one for the accused, the other for the prosecution. Wooden benches with tall backs filled the majority of the space. Just a few beings sat in them: a couple pixies in one, quietly giggling while waving their bony fingers at each other. A couple benches away sat a dwarf, and some being that Christine couldn't identify, that looked like a transformed tree man.

She didn't see Lars sitting up front, though she'd expected him to be there. Was she just a witness? Or was she on trial as well?

A door she hadn't noticed, just beyond the witness stand, opened. He bailiff who came in looked like the same official she'd seen before, with a ram's head and barrel chest. He moved to the center of the courtroom, between the jury and the front desks, then rapped the floor with his great wooden staff.

"All rise!" he proclaimed in that super-sexy voice.

God, she must be more tired than she realized if she thought someone besides a troll was sexy.

"The Honorable Judge Okamby, presiding."

The judge came out the same door the bailiff had. He was mostly human-looking, though his sharp nose and extra-wide grin gave him something of a pixieish look. He looked African-American, with dark skin and curly hair shorn short. He might have come up to the bailiff's chest.

The beings that shuffled out next appeared to be lawyers. They both appeared as human men, with that same buttoned-down appearance. Then came Lars. He'd cleaned up, or at least presented the appearance that he'd showered and changed into fresh clothing, nice white shirt and dark suit. The three of them looked as though they'd been cut out of the same cloth: rich, powerful, privileged: used to getting their own way.

The cut on Lars' face had been healed. She could only hope that he hurt as badly as she did.

After Lars and his two lawyers sat, a third entered the room. She was a petite Asian woman, with her black hair piled high on her head, held there with black hair sticks that had garnets hanging from delicate silver chains. She wore a suit as well, though it was probably the brightest red Christine had seen in a while that wasn't being worn by a Santa Claus stand-in. It was cut beautifully and suited her.

She looked powerful.

Christine knew that Lars and his buddies would discount her for being a woman, as well as for not conforming to the standard dress code.

Christine almost wished she had popcorn so she could enjoy the show more.

With a start, Christine realized the bailiff had called her name. Her troll name, asking for Princess Kizalynn Linumok Te'Dur to take the stand.

Stiffly, Christine rose. She still hurt all over. Her system was working overtime to not only heal all her wounds, but deal with the poisoned claw marks. Her leg still felt fragile, as though it would snap if she put too much pressure on it.

She slowly made her way to the witness stand. Damn it. Stairs. She mounted them one by one. She didn't have to look over at Lars to know that he was smirking.

Stupid demon.

With relief, Christine sat again. Huh. The judge really wasn't fully human, though he appeared to be.

Face on, she caught a glimpse of a magical aura around him.

The bailiff approached the bench. He said something to her in Trollish. His voice sounded even *more* sexy now.

As he raised his right hand during the process, Christine assumed that he wanted her to do the same, to swear some sort of oath about telling the truth. She waited until he was finished before she said, "I'm sorry, I was raised as a human. I don't speak Trollish."

The bailiff nodded at her while Lars gave an aborted snort, giggling at her condition.

Fine. Give her a couple weeks (and oh my god, some books or tapes!) and she'd fix that situation

The bailiff continued smoothly in English. "Please raise your right hand. Do you promise to tell the truth, the whole truth, and nothing but the truth, with your word being your bond?"

"I promise," Christine said. She knew that her word was the only oath she'd need. What sort of oaths did other beings have? Was there any oath that would bind a demon?

The woman lawyer came forward, Mrs. Zhao, as she'd announced herself. She gave Christine a warm smile. "Please tell us, in your own words, what happened this evening."

Christine told them about coming back from Trollville (which caused a restless stir among the jurors, though they knew better than to say anything) and how the shadow demons had attacked her. Then Lars had come.

She told the truth about how she'd constructed the bridge to not bear oath breakers (which caused another stir, big enough that the judge glared in their direction) as well as how she'd forced Lars to change into his true form.

She knew that she was giving the opposing lawyers things they might use against her. She didn't care. She was in the right. The only way to stop Lars was by having him turned over to the courts.

"And what time was this?" Mrs. Zhao asked.

Was that hope in the lawyer's eyes? Was her cat-who-ate-the-canary smile suddenly more smug?

"I have no idea," Christine said. It wasn't as though she'd been checking her phone for the time while she'd been fighting for her life. What did that have to do with anything?

"Are you sure?" Mrs. Zhao asked, fixing her with a stern eye.

What had Christine done wrong? Why was she suddenly being treated like the bad guy here?

"Just before midnight?" Christine guessed. It had been very late in Trollville, she knew that. But she didn't think it had been that late.

"Is there any way you can think of to verify the time?" the lawyer asked. "It's very important," she added.

"Judge, lawyer is trying to lead the witness," one of Lars' lawyers complained.

Mrs. Zhao kept her back to the judge and rolled her eyes at Christine before she turned around and said, "Sorry." She didn't sound sorry at all. "But setting the time is important in all breaks from justice," she continued.

Christine still wasn't sure why, but her aching head finally produced a usable thought. "Can I check my phone?" she asked the court in general.

The judge nodded. "I'll allow it," he stated clearly.

"But—" one of Lars' lawyers tried to object.

"I'll allow it," the judge growled. "She was raised as a changeling. She only knows human ways. She's never been allowed to discover her true nature."

Lars' lawyers continued to scribble madly. Christine would bet that if this ruling came up on appeal, they'd hold this against her.

Did she have some way of knowing what time it was? Was that knowledge buried deep inside the earth? Too late for her to check now. Instead, she pulled out her phone.

As she'd suspected, it had briefly woken up when she'd stepped off the bridge to fight the shadow demons, before Lars had shown up.

"My phone shows that I first returned from Trollville at 11:13 PM," Christine said. "That's the time all the phone messages show."

"And when did Lars Sorgenfrey appear?" Mrs. Zhao asked.

"Shortly after that," Christine said. "I wouldn't leave the bridge. The shadow demons couldn't step onto it. So I called for Lars at that point." She knew she was telling the truth, though she could tell the other lawyers didn't like it much.

"Is there a reasonable probability that you forced Lars Sorgenfrey to revert to his true form before midnight?" Mrs. Zhao said.

"Yes," Christine said firmly. "I didn't want to spend a lot of time fighting him. I was already exhausted and starving. I knew that I'd lose a long protracted battle."

"So the demon Lars came into being before midnight.

Your fight continued well after midnight. We have records of the time you jumped from the bridge onto the ground. You'd been fighting for over an hour," the lawyer said.

Christine merely nodded, not sure if there was a question in there for her or not. No wonder she was so exhausted! She thought longingly of her own bed, though she'd probably take a long, *long* soak in her tub first. Hopefully her water element wouldn't let her drown.

"Did you continue to hold Lars in his demon shape once you'd jumped from the bridge?" Mrs. Zhao asked.

Christine shook her head, then said, "No. How could I? He's a demon. I can't make him do anything on the human plane."

Mrs. Zhao purred. "But you're a troll! Surely you could have held him with your earth power."

"Could I?" Christine asked. "Huh. Didn't think I could do that." She thought about it for a moment, then shook her head. "No, I think you're wrong. I don't have the power to do that. Even if the other creature was standing on good solid earth. I don't have that much sovereignty here, on the human plane."

Could she do it in Trollville? Particularly after she'd been there for a while, and the earth there was accustomed to her and her magic? Possibly...

"So you didn't force him to stay in his demon shape after he left the bridge?" Mrs. Zhao asked.

Christine held onto her temper, but just barely. "I was dying at that point. The shadow demons..." She paused, then made herself continue, "the shadow demons had surrounded me. Beaten me down. I'd fallen, I think, before Lars came down. I wasn't in any condition to hold anyone."

Mrs. Zhao nodded. "Let Princess Kizalynn's injuries be entered into the court record," she intoned.

Well, maybe that angel who'd healed her hadn't been so terrible, not if it recorded all her injuries and they could now be used against Lars.

A paper appeared in front of the judge and on the table in front of Lars' lawyers.

Judge Okamby scowled as he read the paper. He looked up at Christine with much softer eyes. "I am going to pause these proceedings for a moment. Princess Kizalynn, do you need a glass of water or something? Though trolls are exceedingly tough, you were gravely injured and close to death."

"Thank you," Christine said, swallowing around a sudden lump in her throat. Damn it! She couldn't cry, not after all this. Maybe later, when she was back in her apartment and alone. "Some water would be lovely," she added after a moment.

A sparkling glass pitcher of water suddenly appeared in the bailiff's hand. He poured it into the glass that had just shown up on the witness stand.

Christine took a long drink. She suspected that the water had been blessed or something, as regular water wasn't normally this quenching. Even the water in the tollhouse hadn't tasted this good. Finally, after finishing a second glass, Christine nodded at the judge. "Thank you, your honor. I am ready to continue."

"Let this session be in order," the judge proclaimed.

Christine settled in for more questions, preparing herself for what was to come.

~

"I don't even know why we're here," one of Lars' lawyers said. "She admits to forcing my client into his demon form, making him transform. He didn't voluntarily break his parole!"

Christine just barely managed to conceal her snort of derision when Lars tried to make himself look innocent. That look just didn't sit well on his smarmy face.

Watching Lars trying to dig himself out of the hole he'd dug for himself was the only amusement she had. She needed to keep herself distracted as her pains mounted up, one on top of another. Everything hurt. Even her leg throbbed. She was certain the judge was going to scold her soon if her stomach didn't stop its loud grumbling. Christine's amusement (and anger) kept her awake as exhaustion took hold.

She'd been without sleep for more than twenty-four hours. If she had full access to her earth power, she could probably keep going for a while, but she was failing. Fast.

She felt herself jerk back up to sitting. Had she fallen asleep? Damn it.

The judge had just stood up. "Court is now finished. The jury must deliberate. We will reconvene once they've reached their verdict."

Christine barely stifled her moan. She was going to have to wait here? How?

When she looked up, Mrs. Zhao beckoned her forward. "How are you holding up?"

Christine took a chance and told the truth. Or maybe she was just too tired to lie. "Not well," she admitted. "Is there a spare office where I could lie down for a bit? Or at least a cafeteria nearby, where I can get a bite to eat?"

Mrs. Zhao rose instantly. "Come with me," she said. She led Christine back through the door where the judge, Lars, and his lawyers had exited.

This hallway looked like the one out front, like a generic government office. At least this place had carpeting —rough brown with red flecks in it—instead of linoleum. The walls had been painted more recently though still with that same institutional light-gray.

The doors along this hallway were different from the one along the courtroom hallway. Instead of being plain and painted, they were made from real wood, with dimpled glass on top. Mrs. Zhao stopped at a door halfway down the hall. "Come into my office," she said.

It was pretty small as offices went, though it was quite nice. Christine felt comfortable there, probably because bookshelves full of what she figured were law books lined three of the walls. On the wall opposite the door, a huge empty space stood between the two bookcases. Was that a portal? Probably.

A huge desk sat in the middle of the room, like an island floating in the sea. A large leather chair stood behind it, while two smaller chairs sat on the other side.

Christine looked around hopefully, but she didn't see any cot. She felt even less of her earth power here. Or maybe she was just tired, now.

"Sit," Mrs. Zhao ordered, pointing at one of the chairs. "Food will be here shortly," she added after staring off into space for a moment.

Christine sat, happy to take the weight off her leg. The sling around her neck chaffed her, so she took it off. Her arm still hurt. She believed the healing was only superficial, that if she stretched her arm the skin would tear and she'd start bleeding again.

At least Mrs. Zhao didn't want to talk with her. Instead, the lawyer let Christine rest in peace. Moments later (or was it longer and had Christine fallen asleep again?), a tray holding a huge bowl mouth-watering beef stew appeared in midair, along with two bottles of sparkling water.

"Thank you," Christine said, gratefully taking the bowl from the tray. She didn't bother with a spoon, but instead lifted the bowl to her mouth and guzzled the contents.

She'd never tasted anything quite so good: a rich tangy sauce with hunks of tender beef, carrots, potatoes, and turnips. It only occurred to Christine by the time she'd finished that she'd been impolite. She looked up, horrified at her manners.

Mrs. Zhao gave her an indulgent smile. "It won't be long now," she promised.

Christine wiped her mouth with her hand. She looked mournfully at the empty bowl. She'd forgotten her manners once. She couldn't just leave them at the door a second time and lick the bowl clean, could she?

Instead, she handed the bowl to Mrs. Zhao and took the sparkling water in exchange. Like the previous water she'd had, it was cool and refreshing. By the time she'd finished the bottle, she felt, well, almost human. Or trollish. Or something. More recovered, though her arm still felt fragile and all her bruises still ached.

"As I thought," Mrs. Zhao said, directing Christine's attention toward the door. A bright red light flashed urgently beside it. "Time to go back to court," she said. "And hope the ruling is in our favor."

"And how does the jury find the defendant?" Judge Okamby said. Weird echoes of his words bounced around the courtroom, as if they, too, were being recorded somewhere permanent.

Maybe they were. Now that Christine thought about it, she'd never seen a stenographer or court reporter. Did the walls record everything that was said? The whole courthouse was a magical building on some pocket world, after all.

"We find the defendant guilty as charged," the single standing juror said. He looked like a demon, with tendrils of living thorns dripping down his back. He had an elongated, very pale face. He gave Lars a glare.

Demons hated it when they lost.

Christine stifled her chortle of glee. Finally! Something was going her way.

"Your honor, we'd like to postpone sentencing until further consultations," said one of Lars' lawyers.

The judge shook his head. "Denied," he said.

Christine wondered if that was because they were currently short-staffed. Or was it because he really didn't think that anything the lawyers said would change his mind?

She watched the judge, curious as he pulled out an already-prepared piece of paper from a folder.

"Lars Sorgenfrey, I sentence you to return to the maximum security lockup for demons for one hundred years," Judge Okamby said banging his gavel.

Shocked silence filled the room. Christine was certain that Lars' lawyers weren't prepared for *that* sentencing.

"Your honor—"

The judge banged his gavel again. "I have spoken," he said. His voice took on a deeper, more somber tone. "That is your sentence." Again, the words echoed weirdly.

Lars looked as shocked as Christine felt.

She didn't feel sorry for him in the least.

Relief washed over Christine as Lars rose and two beefy guards with short, spiky horns and mere claws for hands came over and took him into custody.

He was really going away. For a good long time.

It wouldn't stop the Great War. However, it would be delayed. Lars and his family would lose enough followers and support that the demons wouldn't pursue the war. Not until they had enough followers that they were certain they could win.

Should she get a restraining order now? Or wait until Lars started bothering her again? He still had it in for her, after all, but he would be gone for a while. Hopefully for the entire century, though she doubted it.

Finally, she had some good news, despite the fact that she was dead on her feet.

"Thank you," she still remembered to say to Mrs. Zhao as everyone shuffled out.

"You're welcome, my dear," Mrs. Zhao said.

For the first time, Christine noticed that the lawyer had, well, what could only politely be described as demon teeth. She shook herself, startled.

Mrs. Zhao gave her more human smile. "Not all demons believe in the Great War," she said softly.

Christine could only blink. She knew the lawyer had meant to be reassuring, but it only bothered Christine more.

Ming, the one who had bound Christine's powers illegally, had said the same thing.

It made her pause and think for a moment. Had she just been manipulated into doing a demon's work? No, everything had been legal. She *hated* dealing with demons. They made her question everything.

With a tired sigh, Christine started the long trek back to her apartment. Though she had her purse, somehow her wallet had been emptied. Stupid demons. Fortunately, she only had the one debit card to cancel. But they'd taken her bus pass, and she was too exhausted to use her powers to float her home. She didn't trust herself with a portal at this point—who knew where she might actually end up?

As soon as Christine stepped from the courthouse, she paused, taking a deep breath of the cool spring air. The sky overhead was a brilliant blue and the winds had softened. Her air element swirled around her. Her earth element pushed at her, too.

What did they want? Could they actually help?

She tried to take another step forward, but they stopped her again.

They couldn't help.

But she wasn't completely alone. She did have family she could call. Friends.

After taking a deep breath, Christine texted her brother.

You still gimping around?

The reply came moments later.

No. Slacker. I'm at work. Where are you?

Christine grinned. It sounded so like her brother. She was glad he was better.

Want to give me a ride home? I'm at the courthouse.

She was surprised at his instant response.

Am on my way. Cavalry to the rescue!

Christine couldn't help but grin, despite how that made the one long scratch on her face hurt.

She didn't have to do everything on her own.

EPILOGUE

Christine guilted Tina into going out to dinner that week, playing on her sense of obligation. (And no, Christine did not like thinking about how much that made her seem like a demon.)

They didn't go to Chef Guido's again, though Christine had been tempted to take her there. Instead, they went to a Basque restaurant just down the hill from Christine's place, close to the park.

Tina put on a happy smiling face, but Christine could see through it to her underlying sadness. Christine didn't bother trying to talk about their Destinies, but instead, chatted about what Trollville had been like, the weirdness of meeting her bio-dad, Christine's anger at the destruction of the cape the king had given her, how Christine was still recovering from her injuries. (She'd had to call into work sick for the entire week, though she hadn't minded too much. She'd caught up on a *lot* of reading, and her to-be-read pile was now half the size it had been.)

When they finished eating, Christine asked shyly, "Could you do me a favor and come with me to the bridge?" It wasn't that she wanted to show off her work. But she had an idea about how to break Tina out of her doldrums without actually bopping her upside the head and telling her to just get over herself.

They walked from the restaurant to the park. The awful snow had disappeared as if it had never been, melting quickly in the warm sun. The air still held a delightful chill, which made Christine happy.

The moon was just peeking over the trees by the time they arrived. The bridge looked magical to Christine. Some of the snow stubbornly clung to the earth here, but then again, it had been piled up much deeper there than anywhere else. The trees that surrounded the meadow were already leafing, bringing with them a fresh scent.

Christine didn't think her earth power would let her grow the grass around the bridge more quickly, though she did suggest it to her element, to see if there was something it wanted to do about healing the earth.

She'd found herself doing that a lot, either making suggestions and letting her elements decide what they wanted to (or could) do, and accepting their suggestions and doing her best to implement them in a way that made sense.

It took more time and effort. But Christine was noticeably stronger when she worked with her elements rather than trying to manage them or force them to do things.

She wouldn't be surprised if the grass did form a carpet here sooner rather than later.

"It is beautiful," Tina said wistfully. "And I can see your influence on it."

Christine beamed at her human sister.

Tina blinked, then smiled back.

Ooppss. It seemed Christine had automatically dropped her human face when she arrived in the clearing. But she was a lot more comfortable in her own skin, now.

"Want to play a game?" Christine asked, asking her earth element and air element to help.

Shadowy demons started to coalesce out of the darkness.

"What are you doing?" Tina asked, instantly alarmed.

"You do have a Destiny, you know," Christine said. She made herself shrink back down into her human size.

The demons loomed around her.

"Watch out!" Tina shouted when the first one reached to claw Christine. Without thought, Tina blasted the beast with magical fire, making it melt back into the shadows.

More demons came. Tina looked dazed but immediately started fighting, clearing the shadows from around Christine. "What are you doing?" Tina asked again as she moved in a blur, smacking one demon in the snout, blasting another to bits with a fire spell, dousing a third in what had to be Holy water (a trick that Christine was really going to have to learn).

"Showing you that you still have a Destiny," Christine told Tina softly.

Tina vanquished the rest of the demons, burning the last three with a fire that nearly scorched Christine as well.

"What were those things?" Tina demanded, marching over to where Christine still stood. She'd dodged a few blows, but had let Tina do the rest of the fighting.

"Memories," Christine told her. "The earth—it remembers the fight that went on here. The demons."

"So they weren't real?" Tina asked, shocked.

"No, no, they were real. If you hadn't banished them, they could have killed me," Christine said. She didn't add that her earth element wouldn't have let that happen. Mind you, it might have let her get beat up some for being stupid. But it wouldn't have let them kill her.

"What kind of a stupid test was this?" Tina asked, angry. She started giving off a dark glow. "Were you just trying to prove how vulnerable you are? How much you needed me to fight?"

"No, no, not at all," Christine said. Damn it! This was all falling to pieces. She reached out her hand. Tina grudgingly took it.

The human's hand felt overly warm against Christine's cool skin. She pushed out some of her calm, the peacefulness her water element brought her.

"What I wanted to say, what I wanted you to know, is that it doesn't matter whether or not you have a greater Destiny," Christine said. "Your true Destiny is to be my friend. To go hang out and eat weird food. To talk about books. To rescue each other so many times that we lose track of who's rescued who more. To be my true sister."

Tina's lower lip started to tremble. "Thank you," she whispered. She dropped Christine's hand and turned away for a moment, gathering herself back together.

Christine gave her the moment, the peaceful night settling in around them.

Finally, Tina turned back to her. "You're right. Destinies don't matter. Friends, and family, do."

"Exactly," Christine said. "Now, you know that just up the hill is a coffee shop that serves this great drinking chocolate? It's thick and rich and comes with tons of whipped cream?"

Tina beamed at her, her bright light finally filling her whole face. "Let's go!" she said, linking arms with Christine. "Lead the way."

Christine knew better than to believe that Tina was out of the woods yet. There would still be dark days, days when she beat herself up for not being more special, more different.

Luckily she had a true mirror to look in, even if that mirror did sport a troll face now and again.

"I promise, Dad, this won't hurt a bit," Christine told her father. He sat on a chair in the backroom of Nikolai's Magical Emporium. The room was still full of the boxes from Mr. Ilcvash, though some of them had been cleared away by the police.

Nik still looked shaken by his ordeal. There had already been a couple of attempts on his life. He'd made more enemies than friends by turning that book over to the special prosecutor. He'd agreed to help Christine figure out what was wrong with her dad.

After a quick examination, Nik had discovered that a worm of the stupid shadows had sneaked into her dad. It had probably come from Dennis, originally.

It made Christine angry just thinking about it. Her dad—the swell guy—would have turned mean and possibly evil if the shadow hadn't been discovered.

It hadn't taken any persuading to get her dad to visit Nik's shop. She'd even had a ready excuse: since her dad was an architect, she wanted him to see the shop and see if he could suggest anything that might help protect it.

All right, it was a lame excuse. Nik had more than enough magical enchantments and protections. But as she'd learned with her fight against Lars, Nik shouldn't underestimate a powerful purely physical attack either.

Dad had exclaimed about all the potions and jars, making the appropriate ooh and ahh noises when Christine showed him some of the magical things.

"So very groovy," Dad said as she completed the tour.

Christine just shook her head. Only her dad still used the word "groovy."

Now, Dad sat, patiently waiting. As the shadow hadn't really taken root yet, it couldn't control his actions. But if Christine had waited even a few more days…

Dad watched curiously as Nick ran a glass globe over his torso. The glass looked empty, and no swirls or color ran through it.

Christine couldn't see anything magical about it either. It appeared to be a plain glass ball.

"Hold it here," Nik instructed Christine.

She reached across and held the globe to Dad's right side, just above his ribs, pressing it into his skin.

Nik let loose with a string of syllables. Christine recognized some of it as one of the demon languages. But there were other words from other languages mixed in there. She couldn't have translated the chant, not even if her life had depended on it. Or even, possibly, her father's life.

She still got the gist of it: it was some sort of spell for drawing something out. She caught the reference to thorns being pulled, as well as the grasping hand drawing the string along.

Nik himself grew much more animated as he spoke, raising his arms up as if entreating the gods. (What gods would a wooden man worship? Would he try to appease the god of fire frequently? Or merely ask for the blessings of water and rain?)

The globe Christine held grew hot. Dad shifted uncomfortably, but he didn't try to brush her hand away.

Christine watched, both fascinated and horrified, as black smoke started filling the once clear globe. It puffed up, completely taking up the space, then condensing, solidifying, into a single black mess.

Nik reached over and pulled the globe up off of her dad's shirt with a loud *pop*. He shook the ball gently.

The leech? Shadow? Thorn? rattled around. It didn't really have a distinct shape. It was more like smoke, shifting constantly into different forms.

Dad gave a low whistle. "I had that inside me? Jeez."

"Well, it had been in Dennis, first," Christine said. "How did it land in you?"

"Beats me." He paused, then said, "You know, in the hospital room, your brother got sick once. Some of the vomit splashed onto me."

"Not onto Mum?" Christine asked, horrified. Did she have to bring Mum in now?

LEAH R CUTTER

"No, no, she was all the way across the room when it happened. Dennis was so embarrassed, couldn't really explain what had happened. He hadn't felt nauseated, then suddenly, upchuck." Her dad chuckled and shook his head. "Had that same look on his face as he did when he'd been just a boy and done something he shouldn't have done."

"I think you're safe," Nik said slowly. "I'll dispose of this. Christine, you need to craft some protection charms, and make sure that everyone in your family wears them."

"I don't—" Christine stopped herself.

She didn't know how to make charms, or do spells, or many other things. However, her elements did.

"I'll see what I can come up with," Christine promised her dad, kissing him on the temple.

"Thank you for taking care of us, darling," he said with a grateful smile.

"And me, as well," Nik added. Christine had offered to spend more time at the shop, to work as protection for Nik. Though Nik had his own magic, whoever came after him would still have to get through her first to get at him. And trolls, as everyone knew, were tough.

"And what about the book?" Christine asked Nik quietly as her dad put on his coat.

Nik shrugged. "The process is moving. Justice moves slowly. But I have time."

Christine thought about that all the ride home. Nik did have time. If his stories were true, he'd been alive for a couple thousand years already.

What were a few pissed off demons when he had a couple thousand more years to live?

Christine knew the Great War hadn't been completely halted, but merely delayed, since she'd just sent one of the primary instigators to prison for one hundred years.

How long would she live? Would she still be there when Lars got out? She kind of hoped so. But she had no idea how long trolls lived. She knew someone she might ask, though.

She didn't need to go back to the bridge every night. She felt drawn to it. The grass was starting to poke above the raw earth. Daisies and other wild flowers would take hold soon, too.

The clearing and the bridge soothed her heart. She felt more at home here than she did in her wonderful apartment.

Which, quite frankly, was starting to feel old and stale. It wasn't as if the walls were closing in on her, but she missed having good solid rocks under her feet. She didn't like the harshly flat walls. She wanted curved tunnels instead. That had been one lovely thing about the tollhouse—while the outer walls were straight as human work, the carved-out area under the hill wasn't.

Could she make herself a home like that one day?

Her earth element stirred.

Oh.

Christine paused. She wasn't about to ask her earth element to make her a house like that right away.

But she knew she could, and it would happily comply.

Early Saturday morning, Christine found herself crossing the bridge into Trollville. The day was hazy and soft rain washed her face. Spring was coming to this land too, possibly a little slower than in Seattle. Then again, this end of the bridge was high in the mountains where it was colder.

Still, the stone path felt so good under her feet. She hadn't been able to repair the black boots the king had given her, but Nik had said to bring them into the shop and maybe she could make a deal with a brownie. Winds played with her hair, and birdsong filled the trees.

She found herself taking deeper breaths here. This wasn't home, not yet, but it so quickly could be.

Smoke rose from the chimney of the tollhouse. Christine wasn't sure why Rodericket hadn't come out to meet her. She hurried along, opening the door to the tollhouse tentatively.

The noise that greeted her made her smile with delight. Trolls filled the room, eating, laughing, talking. Rodericket was busy bustling plates out from the kitchen, followed by Te'Dur.

"Hello!" Rodericket said perfunctorily as he finished putting his plates down on a table of hungry eaters and turned toward the door.

"Oh! Hello! Welcome, my lady! Welcome! Please, please, come in, rest a while," Rodericket said, indicating an empty table close to the door leading away from the bridge.

"Thank you," Christine said. She paused, then looked

at the pile of plates in Rodericket's hand. "No, I don't need to sit. I've already had breakfast. Let me help."

She took the plates from Rodericket's suddenly loose grip and made her way into the kitchen. Three other trolls worked there, two cooks and one dishwasher.

Christine helped carry out orders, cleared tables, set new place settings, even washed and dried a pile of dirty napkins using her water and air elements. She knew that her powers were amused by the menial tasks, but they all chipped in to help.

Finally, a couple hours after noon, the rush died down. Rodericket, Te'Dur, and Christine all collapsed around a table. "Has it been this busy since I left?" Christine asked.

"No, no. Today was the first weekend brunch rush I've had in years," Rodericket said. "It used to be like this, before the scares of the Great War. Rumor has it the fighting's been delayed," he added, turning to Christine.

She gave him a warm smile. "That it might have," she said. "I'm happy for you."

"I can't really pay you, my lady, for all the help you gave me this morning," Rodericket said. "Otherwise I would hire you to come work every weekend."

Before Christine could tell the toll keeper that it was all right, Te'Dur spoke up. "Kizalynn doesn't need the money. She has quite an inheritance."

"I do?" Christine asked, surprised. "I thought the king stripped away all your lands and money when he threw you in prison."

She put her hands over her mouth, knowing that she'd overstepped. It was awfully tacky for her to bring up the fact that her bio-dad was penniless.

But Te'Dur merely smiled at her. "The lands were in my wife's name. He couldn't touch those. So they're now yours."

"I have lands?" Christine said, surprised.

"Maybe even a grand hall or two," Te'Dar said with a wink.

"Won't you also be collecting tolls on your end of the bridge?" Rodericket asked, looking puzzled.

"What do you mean?" Christine asked.

"The fairy bridge is yours," Rodericket explained. "You can control who passes and who doesn't."

"But then I'd have to stay there all the time," Christine said, even though being there often that would delight her. "And how about—" she stopped herself. "Wait. I have money, right? I don't need a human job anymore."

"That's right," Te'Dur said. "And besides, you now have a duty, not just a job. An important one. You guard one of the bridges to the other worlds."

Christine nodded slowly. Her earth element showed her the tunnels it would dig for her under the bridge, as well as here, in the mountains on this side. She could have a cozy space for her books. She would get to read, all the time, between visits from travelers. Her fire element promised a great hearth to read by.

She'd also be able to travel to the other worlds of the *kith and kin* when she felt like it.

"The fairy bridge troll," Christine said slowly.

"The position is yours for the taking," Te'Dur assured her.

Christine finally felt her soul settling. She could watch the bridge, protect it from attack. She could visit her human family whenever she wanted. And she could come here, too. Go back to Trollville. Visit the king. Stop at the colorful marketplace. Get her boots fixed by trolls instead of brownies.

Between this and the work with Nik, she knew she could have the life of her dreams.

"When do I start?" Christine asked.

"You should start now," Te'Dur told her.

Christine nodded, feeling better about her future than she had since, well, forever.

She was finally ready to fly.

READ MORE!

Be sure to read all the books in the Seattle Trolls series!

The Changeling Troll
The Princess Troll
The Fairy-Bridge Troll
The Troll-Demon War
The Troll-Human War
The Troll-Troll War

Available for sale now!

ABOUT THE AUTHOR

Leah Cutter writes page-turning fiction in exotic locations, such as a magical New Orleans, the ancient Orient, Hungary, the Oregon coast, rural Kentucky, Seattle, Minneapolis, and many others.

She writes literary, fantasy, mystery, science fiction, and horror fiction. Her short fiction has been published in magazines like *Alfred Hitchcock's Mystery Magazine* and *Talebones*, anthologies like Fiction River, and on the web. Her long fiction has been published both by New York publishers as well as small presses.

Find Leah's books here.

Follow her blog at www.LeahCutter.com.

Reviews

It's true. Reviews help me sell more books. If you've enjoyed this story, please consider leaving a review of it on your favorite site.

Come someplace new…

Are you a traveler? Do you enjoy exploring strange new worlds, new cultures, new people?

Sign up for my newsletter and I'll start you on your travels with a free copy of my book, *The Island Sampler.*

I will never spam you or use your email for nefarious purposes. You can also unsubscribe at any time.

http://www.LeahCutter.com/newsletter/

ABOUT KNOTTED ROAD PRESS

Knotted Road Press fiction specializes in dynamic writing set in mysterious, exotic locations.

Knotted Road Press non-fiction publishes autobiographies, business books, cookbooks, and how-to books with unique voices.

Knotted Road Press creates DRM-free ebooks as well as high-quality print books for readers around the world.

With authors in a variety of genres including literary, poetry, mystery, fantasy, and science fiction, Knotted Road Press has something for everyone.

Knotted Road Press
www.KnottedRoadPress.com